JUST PLAY PRETEND

JENNIFER ANN SHORE

For Sarah,
Goth author
loves you

ONE

I'm not particularly good at swimming.

I think I could be, if I really wanted to excel at something as taxing and repetitive as synchronized arm and leg movements.

I'd definitely become an expert if, say, a shark somehow found its way into the pool—which would require defying pretty much every law of physics and *logic* of all things—or if I starred in some sort of swimwear commercial.

Exercise as a whole isn't my favorite thing in the world, let alone thrashing my limbs through the otherwise pristine water surface.

But the worst part of it all is definitely that feeling of my lungs wanting to burn or explode or cave into themselves. Not to mention expelling precious air bubbles while I frantically move toward the slightly jutted out edge of the pool, a perfect and somewhat rough surface for clinging.

So, instead, I float.

Well, technically speaking, I break, enter, and *then* float.

The Kellers, our next-door neighbors, installed a pool right around the time we moved in a year ago.

The other families on the street congregated on their front lawns to watch in irritation as the Kellers' construction equipment and our moving truck fought for optimal positions near our driveways.

As I unpacked my belongings, moving them from cardboard box to closet and dresser, I watched it all come together. The workers spent hours in the hot sun, digging a massive hole, then filling it with steel, plumbing, tile, and all the other materials I don't know the names of, and I got to witness it.

So although I don't have any ownership over this body of water, I feel partial to it.

Mr. Keller spent weeks after the final pour of surrounding concrete telling everyone who would listen how lucky they were to get a "top-of-the-line" saltwater pool installed.

He, apparently, won big on one of those gas station scratch cards, and this was how he'd decided to spend the money.

The choice is a little odd, given it's an extravagance for our middle-class neighborhood, but especially since I'm the only one who actually uses it.

And not even for its intended purpose.

There's a break in the chain-link fence separating our yards, so each Saturday night, long after the Kellers have gone to bed, I slip through it. It's become my routine, a ritual to mark the official passing of another week, followed by a long, long sleep-in on Sunday.

The air and the water were both a little chilly when they

first opened the pool for the year back in May, but now that we're firmly into summer, the lukewarm temperature is divine.

I slowly lower myself in, getting just the right reprieve from the stifling air, and sigh in contentment.

I flutter my feet and inhale for buoyancy's sake until after a few tries I hover on the surface. My hair floats out around me like some sort of crown, catching on my forearms as I stretch out completely and fix my gaze upward.

When I finally achieve weightlessness, I let go of the world around me.

I imagine I'm among the twinkling stars and blue-black sky, defying gravity completely as I become part of the constellations, transformed into a beam of light. I feel untethered, even as the sounds of crickets and cicadas attempt to lull me back to Earth.

I've never been much for meditation or ascension, but here, right now, is the closest I get to a higher level of consciousness.

I inhale again, bobbing slightly. I expect that clean, delicious summer scent, so I startle when, instead, the air is clouded with toxins.

The magic that is my midnight ritual dissolves as I breathe in the rancid and coarse smell of tobacco, which immediately sends me into a coughing fit.

My body jerks in surprise.

I sputter as I struggle to plant my feet at the bottom of the pool, then kick myself over toward the shallow end. I get a mouthful of water as I try to catch my breath, making the spasms of my lungs that much worse.

Once my toes touch the spongy material of the vinyl

liner, I stand and rub a hand on my sternum. It's a valiant effort to soothe the irritation and bring my heartbeat and breathing back to normalcy.

"You okay?" The voice is low in volume and timbre, but that doesn't dampen the severity of it in my ears.

The phrasing indicates concern, but the dry way the question is delivered makes it seem like the person isn't actually interested in my answer.

Curiosity overtakes any shred of rational thinking.

I turn slowly, water rippling around me as I take in the person intruding on my serenity.

The only direct and somewhat helpful lighting in our proximity is from the little circles of light embedded in the pool's walls—and the glow at the end of his stupid cigarette.

"Who are you?" I demand through my irritation.

He doesn't answer or move, choosing to simply stare me down.

When a light breeze hits, sending a shiver down my spine and goosebumps up my arms, it's the sign I need to recall my circumstances. My bikini looks laughably immodest compared to his pristine dark jeans and thin, long-sleeved hoodie that's far too much fabric for this heat.

I take a step back, crossing my arms over my chest in irritation and self-preservation. "What are you doing here?"

He fixes his lips in a perfect O, then expels the smoke from his lungs. "Relax," he says coolly.

I don't heed his advice.

Because in the time of his assessing me, the initial

shock of his presence has worn off enough that I'm processing his appearance with a level head.

We seem to be about the same age, but he could easily overpower me if he wanted to.

I'm a short brunette with curves and chipped nails, and he's long, lean, blond, and wearing a watch that seems far too fancy and delicate to be this close to open water.

I can tell just by looking at him, even under the cover of darkness, that he's powerful—not only physically but in the energy he's imbued with.

He absolutely doesn't belong here.

"Look, I don't know who you are or what you want, but you should leave," I say as forcefully as I can.

He doesn't move a muscle as I fidget, choosing to simply watch me in amusement.

I inwardly curse myself for being so vulnerable and unaware, considering I've gone so far as to leave my towel carelessly slung on a tree beyond the fence.

"You're the intruder," he says evenly, flicking the ash away from him. "Not me."

"Excuse me? You have no—" I stop when our eyes meet.

I blink at the slight familiarity in his sharp features.

I haven't spent an overwhelming amount of time with the Kellers, outside of Mrs. Keller—or Marlene as she insists I call her—because the other two people who genetically belong to that last name don't seem to be my biggest fans. Mr. Keller is rarely around, and when he is, his permanent gruffness is more than slightly off-putting. And although our mothers hoped that Tess and I would be fast friends during our senior year, she barely tolerates me.

Still, now studying the guy above me, it's almost laughably easy to recognize the Keller family traits.

The sharp edge of his jaw.

The perfectly straight nose.

The exaggerated cupid's bow on his upper lip.

The color of his eyes is indecipherable at this moment, but I'd be willing to bet all the money I don't have that they're a dark shade of green.

I let out a breath, releasing the tension keeping my body fixed in position, and sink in the water.

I'm not relaxing because of his earlier suggestion or my realization of his genetics—it's simply much warmer to keep my body as submerged as I can.

As the surface hits my chin, I try to recall the conversations I've heard my mother and Marlene share recently.

When their days off from the hospital align, they've been known to kill a bottle or two of wine in our kitchen, and most of the time, I find their banter amusing.

They both work long days and the occasional night as nurses, which gives them plenty of fodder for gossip. But they also chatter about their mutual love for bad reality television or whatever drama is happening with the extended Keller family.

A night or two after I graduated from high school, I recall Marlene mentioning something about Mr. Keller's older brother. He's in the middle of some sort of legal drama with his business, and his son—

"Cole," I say, louder than I intended, as I glance up at him again. "You're Tess's cousin, right?"

He takes a final drag, then bends down to stub out his cigarette on the cement. "Yep."

Thankfully, he has the decency to move his head slightly as he blows out a puff of smoke, meaning the cloud isn't directed toward me.

I'm not exactly thrilled to have been caught in the middle of my ritual, but I'm a little relieved that he's not some sort of perverted serial killer intending to murder me in the water.

If he did, I wonder if the reputation of this pool, this street, this town would change.

Instead of this being the house where someone won the scratch card lottery, it'd be the one with the death pool.

My blood would seep out and mix with the water, getting diluted until the filter could do its job—if it's even possible.

I wonder if the saltwater would preserve my body in this state long enough for the crime scene photos to leave me recognizable?

I can picture it now—the lights, the sirens, and the terrible curiosity at what occurred, along with the horror and devastation of my parents as they watch on helplessly while I'm zipped up in a body bag.

Of course, the evidence would probably be washed away by that point, leaving me as one of those crazy unsolved mysteries.

In tonight's breaking news, the body of child star Alexandra Sutton was recovered...

"And that makes you, what, the girl next door?" Cole's voice snaps me out of the gruesome details in my mind.

I'm forced to recalibrate to my less volatile reality as I lazily paddle around in my neighbors' pool.

I've been many things and many people in my life, but

"the girl next door" isn't a moniker I've ever claimed—not in the traditional sense anyway. I'm not some innocent, doe-eyed girl who falls for the boy whose window is right across from hers.

Plus, I've experienced heartbreak, love, pain, agony, lust, disgust, contempt, and so many other emotions that firmly remove me from the wholesome category.

"How'd you know I live next door?" I ask him curiously.

"Lucky guess," he says as he sits at the pool's edge and rolls up the bottoms of his jeans.

I chuckle, unconvinced. "Yeah?"

He makes a noncommittal noise as his long legs sink into the water. "I was in the kitchen when you snuck in."

"Oh," I breathe.

"This is warm as hell."

"It's not bad," I say, channeling his nonchalance.

In my psych class last fall, I learned about "the chameleon effect," where a person mimics the posture or mannerisms of the people around them.

And it's something I've been doing my entire life.

I like to adopt the traits of the people around me, put myself in their situations and mirror their body language and ways of speaking.

At a young age, I was praised for my ability to do so, but as I've grown, I've used it to stave off boredom and curiosity. I liken myself to all these different personalities to understand the way they live their lives and feel what it would be like to experience it that way myself.

There is also a very real chance that I'm actually just psychotic.

But I guess time will tell.

For now, I fixate on the easy confidence with which Cole holds himself and wonder where it's coming from.

"What are you doing here?" I ask, then I skim my fingertips on the water's surface as I rephrase. "Not like *here*, at this pool, but at this house. I thought you lived in…" I trail off, trying to recall if Marlene mentioned it.

"New York," he supplies.

"City or state?"

He scoffs. "City. Obviously."

"Right." I don't know what's obvious about that, but I don't ask him to clarify. "You're here for a surprise visit, then?"

"Yep."

He sucks his bottom lip in between his teeth and tilts his head back, staring upward at the night sky.

I take it as a gesture of closing himself off from my questioning.

I'm at a loss for what to say next, anyway, so I turn and lie back, leaning my head against the concrete shelf to resume my own perusal of the stars.

At least, I try to, but I'm unable to lose myself in the practice.

It's already a little uncomfortable to use the cement as a pillow, but I'm also viscerally aware of Cole's presence beside me.

We don't even know each other, and now our limbs are submerged in the same water. It feels very intimate, the two of us alone in the dark, and I can't tell if I'm the only one who feels it.

"That's the Big Dipper," Cole says quietly.

Yep, definitely a one-sided thing.

I sigh and turn to the side, taking in his contemplation. "What?"

"There." He gestures upward, attempting to point out the stars with his fingers. "It's actually upside down, but you can see the seven stars right there, they join together."

I squint to try and make it out, and I think I'm successful.

"And that square right there, that's Hercules," Cole continues on. "And Lyra. And Cygnus."

But I don't bother with the sky any longer.

I'm looking at *him*, taking in the sharp edges of his side profile as he easily recites these words that seem so exotic and cool to my own ears.

I'm a little ashamed that after all the time I've spent beneath the stars and the shapes they make, I've never bothered to learn their names.

"You seem to know a lot about astronomy," I say naturally.

"My mom's name was Cassiopeia, so I really had no say in it," is all he offers as an explanation.

I don't miss the past tense.

And while it was a voluntary personal admission, I can tell by his dismissive tone that it wasn't given easily.

I should probably back off, but I can't help it.

"Where's that one?" I ask him.

"Right there," he answers, the edge of his mouth ticking upward. "The little W."

He looks both relieved and miserable as he points it out, which is about as opposite as one can get from the slight arrogance that I picked up on minutes ago.

It's a little jarring, and it's exactly what I don't want during this very sacred weekly ritual, especially with the pressure I'm putting myself under in the days ahead.

I turn and push off from the wall, backing away from him to reclaim the pool for myself.

"I'm going to get back to it," I announce.

"To what, exactly?" Cole asks, raising an eyebrow.

I wing my limbs out, treading water as I move toward the very middle of the pool. "This."

"Do you make it a habit of indulging in midnight swims?"

"Kind of."

"And you think this is the best way to spend your evenings?"

"Don't knock it until you try it."

"Is that an invitation?" Cole drawls, projecting that cockiness again.

I have a split second to decide how I'm going to answer.

I get the impression that he might be the type of guy who is into this kind of stuff. The cat-and-mouse game. The back and forth. The calculated verbal sparring.

It's not that I necessarily have a problem with any of those things, but whenever I meet someone new, I get to set a precedent for how I want to act.

I'm always confident in my own ability to exist, but sometimes I heighten some of my traits, pulling from various characters I've played or goals I have for myself.

Like when my parents had me tag along to my mom's Christmas party, and I had to put on airs of superiority to survive even an hour in a room full of the surgeons she works with. Or how last spring I played up my squeamishness to convince my alpha male lab partner to do all the dissections in class.

I can't help but consider what the typical girl-next-door, the box he's put me in, would do.

Would she flirt with this stranger? Tell him to get the hell away from her? Lecture him on lung cancer and addictive habits?

I shake off those questions, rejecting my own line of thinking.

Because this isn't a charade—it's *my* time to decompress and be my most genuine self, to let go of all the noise and mental weight. I refuse to put him at the center of my thoughts in my own ritual.

"It's whatever you want it to be," I say honestly. "It doesn't matter to me either way."

I can practically *feel* him smirk.

Still, I turn away, and I'm faster, more deliberate, as I float upward, conscious of his eyes on my exposed skin as he lights another cigarette.

<h1 style="text-align:center">TWO</h1>

Against my better judgment and previous display of nonchalance, I peek between the blinds more than I should this morning. It's hard not to, honestly, because I'm half-convinced that last night was some sort of strange dream.

And my bedroom does a great job of enabling this behavior.

The bay window faces directly into the Kellers' backyard. It's the only bedroom in either of the two houses that has a view of the pool, which is why I'm so comfortable sneaking over each weekend. The Kellers are all blissfully unaware and asleep in their rooms in the front of their house, and the same goes for my parents in ours.

The layout leaves no room for Cole, though, so I'm curious as to where they're putting him up. Surely, Tess would never give up her space for a houseguest.

I'm assuming he's either on the couch in the living room, which makes sense given that he saw my arrival, or in the basement, a place Marlene refuses to ever go into herself, citing its overall creepiness.

"What am I doing?" I wonder aloud as I pull back.

I've been in the presence of Cole Keller for less than an hour, and the first thing I do when I wake up is speculate on where he is crashing within the walls of their house?

I'm stepping way over the line of casual curiosity, and I hate myself for it.

I pull myself out of bed, hoping that showering and going through the motions of getting ready for the day—my last true day of a relaxing summer—will keep my mind occupied.

After I feel somewhat put together, I head downstairs, letting out a big yawn as I enter the kitchen.

My parents sit in their usual spots at the table, which is unsurprising because they've sat there every Sunday morning for as long as I can remember.

I take comfort in seeing them there now, even if we're no longer in the house where I grew up.

"Good morning," my mom says brightly, trying her best to not seem absolutely exhausted.

"Morning," I return, rubbing the final pull of drowsiness from my eyes.

"There are muffins on the counter."

These particular store-bought pastries are a mainstay in our household. Their presence usually signals that my mom stopped for groceries on the way home from her night shift, which is prime time for avoiding the weekend crowds, according to her.

"Thank you." I beeline for the container of blueberry muffins. "And good morning to you, Dad."

He chuckles into his crossword puzzle. "It's almost the afternoon now, you know."

"Well," my mom argues playfully, "I haven't slept, and you are still sitting at the table, drinking coffee and doing a puzzle. So we are still somewhat in morning mode."

"Agreed," I say as I sit across from her. "And muffins aren't really a lunch food."

"Napkin," she chides me, sliding the holder closer to my side of the table.

"Sorry," I say with a sigh.

I use it as a makeshift plate, then proceed to crumble my breakfast in my fingertips, creating manageable, bite-size pieces. It's one of those ultra-healthy kinds that has flakes of bran or whatnot in it, so I focus my energy on eating the blueberries.

"So, Allie," my mom starts. "Something interesting happened last night."

I snort because she almost always comes home from a shift with something she deems interesting, but it's usually disgusting.

"Is it going to make me lose my appetite?" I ask tentatively.

She chuckles. "No!"

My parents lock eyes, having some sort of silent *Can you believe this child?* conversation, and I smile at their unspoken words.

I suppose most children are annoyed by their parents, but I find them and their behavior a little endearing. Even if I don't always show my appreciation outwardly, I'm grateful for everything they have done for me.

It's not like I was exactly part of the plan—and my life hasn't exactly been the easiest on them.

The story, as I've been told too many times, is that they met by chance at a coffee shop years and years ago.

My mom was making an insane number of flash cards for her nursing entrance exams, and my dad was coming off an all-night study session for his own finals.

It was one of those absurdly cute rom-com moments where the barista called out a cappuccino, and it happened to be what they'd both ordered. So, of course, they both got up to claim it, each of them promptly offering for the other to take it.

That led to another planned coffee date, then a string of actual dates, and by the time they celebrated their six-month anniversary, my mom was pregnant with me.

I'd think a woman who was trying to get a job in the medical field would have iron-clad rules about the usage of contraceptives, but I'm here as proof of otherwise.

My surprise arrival didn't stop either of them from accomplishing their career goals, though, which meant I tagged along with them almost constantly.

I split my time as a child between the hospital where she worked and the back of various classrooms at the community college where my dad taught.

For the most part, we were your typical middle-class family in Pennsylvania.

Until I met a woman—Rachelle, an acting coach turned agent—who changed my life.

As luck would have it, on her way to a meeting, she accidentally shut her finger in her car door, and it was painful and swollen enough to bring her to the emergency room. She walked away from the ordeal with a bone bruise and a large bill, but she found the five-year-old reenacting her favorite shows in the waiting area to be quite charming.

Things took off from there.

After many dinners and discussions with my parents, I found myself on her roster of young talent.

I didn't exactly understand what was happening at the time, but I was excited to ride in a plane for the first time. I stayed glued to the window as we flew from the mountains of Pennsylvania to the city of Los Angeles, where I landed a string of appearances in commercials.

After a year spent getting more comfortable memorizing lines, I landed the lead role in a family movie titled *Wanda*.

It was a small indie project about a young girl who is sent off to live with a standoffish uncle after the unexpected death of her parents. She's lonely and isolated at school, and as she gets bullied on the playground, she discovers she has magical powers. As she comes into her abilities, she makes friends, overcomes the death of her parents, and finds herself.

Overall, *Wanda* is a pretty sappy story, but for reasons I still don't entirely understand, it took off.

I had a blast while doing it. I thought it was kind of a fun way to spend a summer, memorizing lines and performing in front of a camera while my mom fawned over a few of the A-list actors in the movie.

Back then, red carpets weren't the big affairs they are now, with live television interviews and thousand-dollar dresses. One of the few pictures we've managed to hang in the new house is of me standing in front of a movie poster with my own face on it, wearing a hand-me-down dress and a gigantic bow in my hair.

And to say that the movie was a smashing hit would be an understatement.

I was flown out multiple times in the school year for interviews and landed other gigs, like guest spots on two television shows, including my mom's then-favorite medical drama.

In the years after I quit the industry, I barely gave it any thought—mostly out of self-preservation—and felt happy to be a somewhat normal teenager.

At least, until last year happened.

When my dad got a new job at the big university in Pittsburgh, it came with a nice pay raise and a few other perks, including the opportunity for me to attend college there for free once I graduated.

I wasn't exactly thrilled at the idea of moving school districts for my senior year, but I saw the long-term gains of it.

My family relocated only an hour drive from where I grew up, so I imagined my best friend, my boyfriend, and me all taking turns meeting in the middle.

Being separated from my lifelong friends twelve months early didn't seem like such a big deal at the time—mostly because the idea never occurred to me that things would change.

I definitely never thought that said best friend and boyfriend would share a pack of wine coolers at a party and end up fooling around, resulting in the immediate breakup of both my relationship and that friendship.

Even worse, the fast turnaround of selling our house

barely gave me any time to adjust, and scheduling my classes was a bit of a nightmare. I got shoved into the remaining slots in classes and the available electives, which brought me back to the performing arts.

I wanted to rebel against it, to beg my parents to home-school me or do anything other than go back to what I'd left behind years ago, but I kept my mouth shut.

They were going through enough with adjusting and rebuilding our life here, and I didn't want to compound my issues on top of it.

The theory of the class was interesting. I learned about scriptwriting and the technical side of production, but a large chunk of our grade hinged on taking part in the fall play.

There was no rule about exactly what our roles had to be, and I approached it all very tentatively.

I stayed behind the scenes, choosing to work on hair, makeup, and costumes, cautiously watching it from afar, taking it all in.

And slowly but surely, I fell in love with all of it.

The feeling of flipping on those bright lights.

The buzz of excitement from the audience taking their seats.

The nervous energy before the curtain rises.

The true escapism only that type of pretending can bring about.

It was so different from film and television acting, and it scared the hell out of me for several reasons. I stuck with the class, and despite my reservations, I got volunteered for a very small background role—with no lines, thankfully—in the spring play.

"Guess who came into the ER at the beginning of my shift yesterday?" My mother's eyes flash with excitement. "Just take one guess."

"You?" I retort smartly before dropping bits of muffin into my mouth.

She shakes her head but doesn't lose her enthusiasm. "Joe Morales!"

I nearly choke. "Is he okay? What was he doing there? Is everything set for tomorrow? Did something bad happen?"

"Yes," she says quickly. "Totally fine. And he said I could tell you he was in."

"No HIPAA violations here," my dad jokes.

"Of course not!" Mom scoffs before smiling slyly at me. "He was even more charismatic than Marlene described."

After Marlene elbowed me into admitting I was taking an interest in performing again, she took it upon herself to call her old buddy Joe to see what he was working on.

He's a Tony Award-winning actor and noted theater director who moved back home to Pittsburgh a few years ago, wanting to make a name for himself here as a big fish in a smaller pond.

Each summer, he runs a program at the local theater for young performers.

It's on a little bit of an expedited schedule, starting with him and the nearby wannabe writers of the world who meet for a week to come up with an idea and actually write the script. When that's finished, the next six weeks are dedicated to casting, blocking, memorizing, sewing, fitting, prop creation, and every other thing imaginable. Finally, the entire production takes place on one big, fabulous opening night in the middle of August.

It took some coaxing on Marlene's part, but I agreed to sign up.

My parents were surprised by my interest but supportive because, if nothing else, it's giving me something to occupy my days between the end of high school and the start of college.

I, however, am equally as excited as I am terrified of what this program brings.

"So what happened?" I ask my mother, fishing for more information. "He just strolled into the ER and started talking?"

"His daughter broke her finger playing softball. She forgot to put her glove back on, she said. And we got to chatting while waiting for the X-rays to come back."

I really wish she'd spill the details faster, but I withhold my irritation. "Chatting about what?"

"Well, at first we were catching up about the Kellers and family stuff."

"Did he tell you anything about the play or who else is auditioning or anything at all?" I press.

Tomorrow, we'll all meet for the official kickoff of the program. The entire group is going to gather in the old theater I've driven past hundreds of times, and the writers will reveal the script and further details before the official casting call.

I imagine it will be a typical first day, with introductions and an overview of the script, but I'm ready for all of it.

"He didn't say anything of consequence that I can recall," my mother says.

I can practically feel myself deflate as I polish off the rest of my stupid muffin crumbs. "Oh."

"But he did say he's very eager to meet you."

"Eager?" I clarify, forcing myself to stay cool. "Is that the exact word he used?"

My mom chuckles. "I was a little preoccupied with his daughter's injury, but yes, I believe that's what he said. And he's looking forward to your audition."

I blink. "Audition?"

"I think we all assumed you'd be going for a part," she says, a little surprised.

My dad eyes me curiously. "Aren't you?"

I haven't exactly decided what I want to do yet.

And I'm running out of time.

"I guess I should see what the play is before I decide what I want to do," I say as a deflection.

"You're going to do great, Allie," my dad encourages, reaching over to gently squeeze my hand. "Don't worry about anything."

"I'm not stressed," I tell him easily. "I'm…processing and plotting. There's a clear difference."

His eyes brighten. "Sounds like you're fixing to take over the world."

"Who says I'm not?" I ask, letting a smile spread across my face.

"Good answer," my mom says as she stands and drops her empty cup in the sink. "Well, I'm going to take a quick nap. Allie, can you please run this bottle of wine over to Marlene for me?"

"Isn't it a little early for wine o'clock?" I ask, mocking the name they've given their little happy hours.

"She and Kevin are going to a party tonight, so I offered to pick up an extra bottle for them while I was at the store this morning."

"Got it," I say, tossing my trash in the bin.

On occasion, my mom and Marlene let me share a small glass with them.

It makes me feel more chic to drink from the fancy stemware, but I actually find the taste abhorrent. I can only hope that someday in the future, I'll have the type of refined palate that can pick up on notes of chocolate and oak.

In this moment, though, I'm content to trace the label with my fingertips.

"Thank you," my mom calls as I step through the back door.

"Uh-huh," I return, waving over my shoulder with the bottle of wine.

Just like I did twelve hours ago, I move between yards.

But instead of giving away my secret passage in broad daylight, I walk around to the front of the house and knock on the door.

This neighborhood is somewhat charming, with one- and two-story homes and well-kept yards. I haven't found the other residents on our street to be overtly friendly, but I earn the occasional wave or smile when cruising down the street in my car.

I inhale the floral scent from the tiny but thriving garden to my left, smiling at the little petunias and hibiscus flowers.

Marlene has given me multiple lectures on the best ways to care for them, and as much as I appreciate the sight, I can't say I've retained any of the information she's shared.

"Lex," Marlene greets me enthusiastically, welcoming me inside with a wave of her hand.

She's always, without asking or letting me clarify, called me by that short nickname.

"Allie," which my parents have always used, seems childish in comparison to this moniker. "Lex," in my opinion, is somehow more dignified but less of a mouthful than all the syllables of "Alexandra."

And I love it.

So much so that I've considered adopting it as my college persona. We as humans only get a few chances to completely reinvent ourselves, and I think if there's a time to get adopting of a nickname, it's when I'm going to have to introduce myself to roommates and classmates.

I imagine how I'd act when my name is called for attendance, correcting them from the mouthful of my name to those three little letters, and even the idea makes me smile, pretending I'm so sleek and mature and mysterious.

"Here," I say, placing the bottle gently on the counter. "I came to drop this off for you."

"Thanks, love," she returns.

"My mom said you needed it for tonight?"

"I need wine every night," she tells me flippantly. "But yes, Kevin and I have a thing with some of his dealership friends."

I raise my eyebrows in question. "Fun?"

"The opposite of," she insists with a sly grin. "Which is why the wine is imperative."

I withhold a smile as I take in the massive pile of rollers holding her auburn hair in place.

Marlene is a firecracker personality-wise, but in the looks department, I could drop her into any old Hollywood movie, and she'd fit in just fine.

And as lame as it makes me feel, I think she's the only actual friend I have in this town.

"You feeling good about tomorrow?" Marlene asks.

"Yes," I tell her, forcing the confidence I couldn't muster in front of my parents. "Very much ready to get going."

That statement, at least, is true.

She purses her lips for a moment before she saunters to the other side of the kitchen. "You look like you're in need of some sugar, Lex."

"Always."

With my mom force-feeding me healthy food every chance she gets, Marlene makes it a point to offer me candy or other sugary treats whenever she can. The Kellers have an entire candy drawer in their kitchen, so it's almost rude if I don't partake.

It absolutely contributes to my fondness of her—and the two cavities I had to get filled last spring.

"Sour today?" Marlene asks as she pulls out a bag, giving me a knowing look before handing it over.

"Yes, please," I say excitedly.

I tear the package open and immediately pop a few of the cute little coated watermelons in my mouth. My teeth practically scream at the amount of sugar they're bathing in, but my brain appreciates the jolt.

"You're the best," I tell her.

My left eye twitches at the bitterness on my tongue, and she laughs loudly at the sight.

"Oh, I know," she says, shaking her head.

Marlene checks out the bottle of wine my mom selected as a thumping sound from the basement picks up, indicating someone is coming up the stairs.

I have three guesses as to who is responsible for the noise, but I don't think I need them.

I swallow another lump of candy and lean against the counter, trying to fix my face back to normal and come across casually.

The wooden door creaks loudly on its hinges before swinging open, and the force of the motion smacks it against the fridge.

Cole emerges from the dark, dusty depths of the basement with two plastic containers in his hands, then sets them on the kitchen table.

I take him in as I bat away my watery eyes, the lasting consequence of ingesting so much sour candy at once.

"This is it, then?" Marlene asks.

He brushes his hands together like he's happy to wash them of this task. "Yes."

When he turns, I get the first glimpse of Cole Keller in daylight.

And I am not disappointed.

It's not his presence that startles me—because in the back of my mind, I knew he would be here this morning—but all the details I missed out on last night.

I am both shocked and distressed at how I practically swoon at his height and mussed blond hair, but taking in his green eyes, I don't just see cockiness or stubbornness or any surface-level emotion.

I see something deeper and slightly broken, like he's projecting the sharpness of his gaze, the overall severity of his eyes, and his confident posture to hide what a mess he is inside.

And that is more alluring than all the other things.

"Turn," Marlene orders her nephew.

"What?" Cole asks.

Marlene twirls her fingers around, indicating how he should move.

He doesn't drop his confused expression as he complies, holding up his hands and slowly moving in a complete circle.

I unabashedly take him in, wondering what role he'll play in this life. He has the kind of demeanor that would appear at home on a runway just as easily as it could aid him in swindling money from unsuspecting rich widows.

I'd probably be content to watch him do any of it.

I blink at my own inner dramatics and force my attention on Marlene, wondering if I'm *that* obvious with revealing my thoughts, but when I see how she's scanning his clothing, I realize that is far from the case.

Marlene steps forward and pulls a cobweb from the back of his head, wincing as she flicks it out the window.

"Ugh," she groans before continuing her perusal. "I don't see any other cobwebs or lingering creepy-crawlies on you."

"Glad to hear it," he says flatly before running a hand through his hair.

I've already thrown out my inner self-respect *twice* since

I've woken up this morning to be a proverbial puddle at this man's feet.

To combat my disgust at myself, I toss another handful of sour candy into my mouth, wishing the burn on my tongue did a better job of distracting me.

"Cole, this is Alexandra." She waves her hand between the two of us. "And vice versa. Lex lives next door, and Cole lives in New York, but somehow the fates have brought you both to this very kitchen in time to help me out."

I so desperately want to be the type of girl who doesn't cower in awkward moments, who comes up with witty things to say and casually flicks her hair over her shoulder as she gets stared at.

Manifesting doesn't always work in real life, but in this case, playing pretend does.

And so I become that version of myself.

I inhale, filling my lungs with air and my mind with the idea that I have no reason to falter under any circumstance.

"Well, if the *fates* demand that we help you, then I certainly can't say no," I retort with a laugh.

"That's the attitude I like," Marlene says, making my heart swell.

"Good."

Because I've decided it's here to stay.

At least temporarily.

"Now, for more help." Marlene steps into the hall and pivots her body toward Tess's bedroom. "Tess! Get your cute butt out here."

I approach the table confidently, eyeing the fabrics contained in the clear plastic. "What do you need us to do? Take these to the car?"

"Not yet. First they need to be sorted." She pops the lid on one of the containers. "God, I don't even know what's in these."

I hold up a baby blue ballgown with puffed sleeves. "What is this for?"

"Joe knows that my parents were hoarders, and he's looking for some donations to the costume department. I told him I'd look to see what would work."

"Is this a hint at the play topic?" I ask quickly, gripping the dress almost desperately.

"No cheating," she says.

I exhale. "Fine."

"That right there is my prom dress," Marlene says proudly, then digs into the bin again and pulls out a sash and crown. "And I was the queen."

"No way." I glance up at her again, taking in her pristinely applied makeup and wide smile. "Then again, I'm not surprised."

She moves to put the crown on her head, only to realize she still has all the rollers in place, then chuckles at her own forgetfulness.

Cole moves to my side, leaving only an inch or two between us, and begins sorting through another container.

I breathe a sigh of relief at the lack of cigarette smoke around him.

He doesn't offer any emotion or snarky comments as he admires a few musty band shirts, taking his time to examine each one carefully.

I watch in my peripheral vision as he traces the logos and tour dates, then folds up each individual clothing item and places them gently on the tabletop.

I clear my throat and tilt my chin up. "So, Cole, how long are you—"

A loud bang from the direction of Tess's bedroom catches our collective attention, and she curses loud enough that I can clearly make out the words.

"Tess!" Marlene yells as she wrestles with her hair. "Language!"

"Sorry," she calls, not sounding an ounce apologetic, as she opens her door.

Tess sprints out, getting a running start to better slide across the wood floors in her socks. She stops herself by crashing into the kitchen counter and groans, then gapes at us all working in tandem.

"How many times have I told you not to do that?" Marlene asks, but there's no venom in her tone.

Tess sighs. "Many."

"You're going to make the floors slippery for the rest of us." Marlene shakes her head. "Heaven forbid if your father slips and falls. It'll take all of us to get him back up."

I hide my smirk at that mental picture of the towering and slightly terrifying Mr. Keller falling like he's some cartoon character who slips on a banana peel.

"Yeah, yeah," Tess says, gaze still locked on the scene before her.

I'm not sure if she's more shocked to see me in the room or at how we've taken over the kitchen.

"Nice of you to join us," Marlene says. "Some assistant stage manager you're turning out to be."

"You're the assistant stage manager for the theater program?" I ask, dumbfounded.

"Yeah," Tess answers in a clipped tone. "What's going on here?"

"We're donating some old things to the costume department at the theater," Marlene says, humming as she holds up a bright orange slip dress. "And Cole, here, is going to volunteer on set production this summer."

"The entire summer?" Tess says with wide eyes. "You're staying here for a while, then? Longer than last time?"

He nods, not looking up from the task at hand.

I watch as Tess fixes her features back into the slight scowl that seems to permanently reside on her face while in my presence.

"We're glad to have you here, Cole," Marlene says as brightly as she can. "As long as there are no dangerous stunts being pulled that will send my daughter to the emergency room with a broken arm, we should be fine."

"Mom, that was like eight years ago," Tess reminds her with an annoyed tone.

Marlene brushes past it to narrow her eyes at Cole. "And no more smoking, either," she adds.

"You *smoke* now?" Tess asks Cole incredulously.

He frowns and shrugs. "Not anymore, I guess."

"Come help us," Marlene encourages her daughter.

"Hard pass," Tess says, eyeing the pile of shirts Cole attends to. "I'll take these, though."

Her mother glares at her. "Tess Marie."

"What?" She holds the pile to her chest protectively. "Consider it my fee for all the unpaid work I'm doing for *your* friend this summer."

I assume it's somewhat normal banter between the two

of them until Marlene's face flushes, and she puts her hands on her hips.

"I'm just about sick of this attitude," Marlene snaps, something I've never witnessed until now. "You and your girlfriend had a big fight, and it's awful. Heartbreaking. But it doesn't mean you can walk around all high and mighty and moody."

"Mom," Tess says, teeth gritted in a warning tone.

My eyes widen at the truth that just got dropped.

I thought *I* was the special one responsible for her attitude.

"Right, right, boundaries and company and all that," Marlene says, rolling her eyes. "But you'll be the one who'll take this over to the theater later today. You can take my car while your dad and I are out."

Tess's smile starts to form.

"And that's it," Marlene adds quickly. "To the theater and back. Nowhere else. You hear me?"

"Yes," Tess groans.

"I can take them for you," I say in a gentle tone, not wanting to rile up Tess even more. "I don't mind."

"No, no, it's okay," Marlene says. "You go off and enjoy your Sunday, Lex. After all, your summer schedule is about to get very busy."

I smile at her as I place the garments back in the container. "I hope so."

Before I step away completely, Marlene pushes the bag of sour candy into my hands. "Don't forget these."

"Thanks, Marlene. I'll see you later."

She's the only one who acknowledges my presence as I head out the front door.

THREE

There are few things in this life I hate more than being late.

And, of course, today of all days is the one when I oversleep.

Somehow I managed to knock my phone to the floor in the middle of the night, and I didn't hear the vibrating sound of my alarm against the carpet.

Instead of a slow awakening and a few rounds of snooze, my body jerks awake when I hear the garage door open, signaling my mom's departure.

I curse as I jump out of bed and dash to my bathroom, running through my shower and the rest of my routine much faster than I had hoped.

If my life were a movie, I would have had a gentle wake-up, soaked in the tub, then perfected my makeup before sitting down to a glorious breakfast spread. But here, in this reality, I go heavy on the dry shampoo, only make time for mascara, and grab a granola bar as I run out the door.

To be fair, I am still *technically* on time.

But it has been ingrained in me by my very punctual parents that if you're not early, you're not on time, and if you're not on time, you're late.

"Allie," my dad calls as I take my keys off the hook.

"I'm running behind," I reply quickly.

He steps into the hallway and pulls me in for a hug. "Good luck," he says before pressing a kiss on the top of my head.

I relent and squeeze him extra tight before I let go. "Thanks, Dad."

"Cole and Tess are already waiting for you," he tells me as he glances out the front window.

"What?" I ask, a little panicked.

These are absolutely not the companions I need right now in my frazzled state…

Tess, who hates me.

Cole, who…exists.

"Didn't your mom mention that Marlene asked if you'd chauffeur them to the theater?"

"No," I groan.

He blinks at my dismay. "Is there a problem?"

"No, no," I say quickly, then follow it up with the flash of a smile that I doubt meets my eyes. "I'm just a little disoriented at the moment."

"Totally understandable." He nods a few times. "You know, this might be the first time this summer you've been up before noon."

I smile at him and release a breath. "Maybe that's part of the problem."

"Well, get going," my dad says as he nudges me.

"Right, right," I say, then shut the front door behind me.

I press the unlock key on my Jeep.

The beep causes Tess to jump and glare at me, while Cole simply gives me a glance that reveals absolutely nothing about what he's thinking.

"Ready?" I ask as I approach.

"Shotgun," Tess says immediately, earning an eyebrow raise from Cole. "Oh, right. You don't know this because you're a fancy New Yorker. See, here in the sticks, we drive our cars from place to place."

He rolls his eyes. "We do have cars in the magical land of Manhattan."

"No," his cousin corrects as we climb in. "You get *driven* around the magical land of Manhattan. You don't have to do the actual driving. There's a difference."

"Seems pretty similar to what is happening now, actually."

As soon as I turn the key, Tess adjusts the knob on the air conditioning to full blast even though it's not even that hot out right now.

She points all the vents to blow directly on her, and it's annoying how comfortable she is in my space. Worse, the effortless banter between Tess and Cole makes me feel like an outsider in my own car.

And I'm already feeling off-kilter enough this morning.

I don't need to expend the energy to try to fix it—I just need to get to the theater on time.

But, of course, my low gas light flickers on just as I turn onto a busy street.

I check the gauge, noting that it's too much of a risk to

not fill it, and I surrender to the fact that nothing is probably going to go right this morning.

Maybe this is just karma reeling itself back in, holding steady until I *really* need things to go my way.

At least, that's what I reassure myself with.

"You've got a nice car," Cole says to me directly, gaze meeting mine in the rearview mirror.

"Thanks," I say, slightly taken aback.

"You'd be surprised how many people want these types of cars with the winters we have," Tess grumbles. "So impractical."

She flicks the removable hardtop roof, then opens my glove compartment, rifling through my papers.

"Do you mind?" I ask her as I grip the steering wheel in irritation.

"No," she says before turning back to address Cole. "And my dad got her a good deal at the dealership, though."

"It's true," I confirm needlessly.

"So, if Uncle Kevin is a used car salesman, why hasn't he sold *you* one?" Cole asks her.

I've been wondering this myself, actually, since I'm stuck being their chauffeur and the fact that Marlene seemed pretty adamant about Tess not doing any superfluous driving yesterday.

"Right after I got my license, Gabriela and I—" Tess stops and lets out a massive sigh. "Long story short, I totaled my car, and my parents are still pissed."

"That sucks," Cole says.

She nods. "It does."

"Good thing you're going off to school and won't need one anyway."

"I guess." Tess sits back, tapping her fingers on the window before doing a double take. "You're going the wrong way. It would have been faster to take a left back here."

"I'm almost out of gas," I say neutrally.

She huffs like it's some great inconvenience to take a detour.

I get it, but I don't appreciate her attitude.

"Can I?" Cole leans forward, gesturing to the radio dial.

"Sure. Thanks for asking permission."

I give Tess my best side-eye, and she sulks as some trendy rock song blares.

It's a little too loud for any conversation, but I don't mind. It's like we have a soundtrack to cruise along to, even if it's just to the gas station that's ten minutes from my house.

When I stop the car in front of a pump, we all get out.

I swipe my debit card and begin to fill up the tank as Cole and Tess head inside to the little convenience store. And by the time they get settled back in the car, I've balled up the receipt and sanitized my hands multiple times, trying to cleanse my skin of any residual gas fumes.

"Pass me the goods, will you, Cole?" Tess asks, holding her hand behind her.

He buckles himself in, then rifles through the plastic bag. "Here," he says, pulling out a family-size portion of peanut M&M's.

"Thanks," she says before she drops a bunch of them in her mouth.

Cole cracks the window as I pick up speed.

"Please don't smoke in here," I say politely, anticipating his next move.

He smirks. "I wouldn't want you to get into a coughing fit and veer us off the road."

"Or maybe that's what we need," Tess mutters before pouring another generous amount of chocolate candies directly into her mouth. "A quick, painless death instead of the slow one we'll be undergoing for the next two months."

Cole shakes his head at her. "Tess. Morbid."

I wonder if Cole feels the same way Tess does about the program, but I don't think I'm in a good enough spot with either of them to ask more about their thoughts on the topic. I refocus on the immediate concern.

"I'm serious," I reiterate to him, flicking my gaze between the street ahead and the rearview mirror. "No smoking in here."

"I heard you the first time," he says evenly as he pulls out several packs of gum.

My expectation was cancer-causing chemicals, but the reality is sugar-coated nostalgia.

"Is that Bubble Tape?" I ask incredulously.

"Aunt Marlene doesn't want me to smoke," Cole says simply.

"And you're just going along with it?" The words tumble out of my mouth. "Cold turkey, easy as that?"

He shrugs. "It's not important."

It makes me curious as to what is.

"Can I get a tear from that?" Tess asks. "I didn't even know this was still sold in stores."

I don't think it will mix well with all the chocolate she just ate for breakfast, but I'm not in a place to judge candy consumption, nor do I feel like voicing that opinion.

"Sure," Cole says, tossing the pink package up to her.

She fumbles with it slightly, gets her own piece, then drops the round container in the cupholder between us.

I ignore the fact that she doesn't offer me any because my curiosity is still fixated on Cole, even as I weave through the morning traffic.

"I don't mean to offend you," I hedge.

Cole crackles the gum between his molars. "That's usually what people tell you before they say something wildly offensive."

"Fair," I agree, tapping my thumbs on the steering wheel. "But I'm wondering why you're so readily giving up a habit. You don't seem like the type to do what everyone tells you."

He sits back against the seat, letting his head lull against the rest. "I'm not old enough to buy my own."

"I can get them for you," Tess offers after popping her bubble. "You only have to be eighteen here."

"How do you know you have to be twenty-one to buy cigarettes in New York?" Cole asks.

Tess shrugs as she concentrates on not breaking her next one. "I just do."

"I'll pass anyway," he continues. "Aunt Marlene is nice but kind of terrifying when she wants to be, and she'd kill me if she found out. Plus, I'm not trying to do anything that's going to get me kicked out of the house."

"Oh," I say because I don't know what else to.

The silence settles over us all for a beat, and Cole turns

up the music once again, filling the hole in the conversation.

Throughout the school year, I was almost desensitized by the idea of performing enough to not have a complete breakdown on stage when it was my turn to step on it.

But now, after weeks of lazing around my house, just *looking* at the building as I pull into the parking lot creates a ball of anxiety in my stomach.

I was so concerned with being on time that I almost forgot about what was actually expected of me when we arrived—and how much I'm looking forward to this production.

And now, I'm a nervous wreck.

I pull into the parking space and try to put on a false front. My hands shake slightly as I take in several people milling about, which means that although we're definitely not early, we're also not late like I feared we'd be.

I have tunnel vision as I get out of the Jeep and make for the theater.

It's one of those old and slightly grand structures of decades past. The ceiling is high and adorned with gold leaves and red accents, which match the carpets and cushy seats. The cold artificial air doesn't do anything to hide the slightly stale scent of it all, but I don't think I mind either too much.

I walk quickly and take a seat a row behind where most of the others have congregated. I'm not in the mental place to make small talk, and I also want to get a holistic view of the people and the room itself.

I'm slightly startled when Tess sits beside me, followed by Cole. Thankfully, they both remain just as silent as I do, taking it all in and giving my mind free rein to let the anticipation build.

I check the time on my phone again and again, waiting for Joe Morales to make an appearance.

"Chill with the neuroticism," Tess finally snaps, hitting my shaking thigh with her fist.

"Gah!" I scowl as I shift to the other side of my seat. "You're freakishly strong."

"I don't think your leg has stopped shaking since we left this morning, which honestly isn't very comforting for a passenger," she hisses. "Give up the whole nervous act. It's exhausting."

I frown. "I'm not—"

"You're the most famous person here," Tess says simply. "You shouldn't have a problem."

Cole leans forward to get an unobstructed view of me, eyes scanning my likely horrific posture. "You're famous?"

I smooth down the front of my shirt dress, mentally preparing for what's to come.

For months after *Wanda* released, it was all anyone my age could talk about, and I couldn't go anywhere without seeing the movie poster with my face on it or overhear someone talking about it.

It all happened so fast—the rise of stardom and then the crash and burn.

At my old school, the one where I had all the same classmates for my entire life, no one cared about my past career. They found it boring and uninteresting; although, it was sometimes a funny anecdote at parties or sleepovers.

All last year, at my new school, I got bullied for it. It took me a long time to put that specific word to the behavior. But after the hundredth random snide comment in the hallway and someone approaching me, mockingly, asking for my autograph, I realized that was what was happening to me.

I can't say it was as gutting of a feeling as the day I decided to quit acting, but it hurt nonetheless.

I was mostly left alone for my actual theater class, but outside of it, some of my fellow classmates only addressed me as "Wanda." They also regurgitated some of the most popular—and slightly cringy—quotes back to me and played video clips I wish I could scrub from the internet.

"Hardly," a sneering voice says.

I glance up, taking in the familiar sight of Esme Carrington, with her modelesque stature, delicate features, and talent that landed her the lead role in all the plays at school.

It appears that in the month since we've graduated, she still hasn't moved past the idea that I'm a threat. She seems unable to accept I'm the furthest thing from competition she has here, even though I told her at least twice that I'm just trying to enjoy the craft, not steal anyone's spotlight.

"I'm Esme," she says, plastering on a smile and brightness that makes me want to strangle her. "Are you auditioning, too?"

The question is directed toward Cole, whose lack of response has the unfortunate side effect of urging her to continue speaking.

"Well, I guess it's not technically an audition for me. I had the lead in last year's school play, both in the fall and spring productions."

"Impressive," Cole deadpans.

She laughs, somehow managing to swipe her tongue over her top lip in a seductive way at the same time.

Cole offers her a bored expression before blowing a massive gum bubble, earning a look of confusion from Esme but a chuckle and an elbow from Tess.

"Welcome!" The booming voice of Joe Morales fills the auditorium without the aid of a microphone. "I repeat, welcome to the tenth annual Morales Play Festival, the community-led theater event that *you* all make possible, but I get to take all the credit for."

The majority of the people in the room burst out laughing, finding his self-deprecation and humility adorable.

I'm not among them.

It's not that I don't buy it, but I've been waiting far too long to find out the details of the play to appreciate the introduction.

"Sutton, stop," Tess hisses beside me.

I stop all my fidgeting immediately, not even realizing I started shaking my legs once again.

Esme turns around briefly to glare at us, and her sneer is a good reminder of exactly why I'm here.

I don't want to get in some catty fight or to play the part of the nervous, washed-up actor who is desperate for validation or another shot at being the star. There's nothing for me to prove here, no redemption arc for my character or a comeback to a career I lost a long time ago.

I'm here to enjoy it, whatever that means.

"...and so, after all that," Joe says as I refocus my attention on him, "I am very happy to be the one to finally announce this year's summer play."

I lean forward in anticipation, and it appears the shift in my outward demeanor doesn't earn me any additional comments from Tess.

"This year's play is *In Wonder*, a modern take on *Alice in Wonderland*."

The noise of conversation increases immediately, the room buzzing with chatter and speculation.

Esme squeals in delight, and it's easy to understand why. She's the embodiment of Alice, with her flowing, blonde hair and bright blue eyes.

I can even almost picture her at a damn tea party.

"Hey, hey, not finished yet," Joe says, patiently waiting for the room noise to quiet once again. "This isn't your average Lewis Carroll tale. It is still rooted in Wonderland, and guided along by the White Rabbit, but it's a little grittier, and a lot darker. Our sweet, unsuspecting Alice isn't exactly who you think she is."

There are a few *oohs* and *aahs* in the audience in response.

"Now, as part of our introductory day, we're going to ask you all to split off. Talent, stay seated. Production, head backstage. Anyone who doesn't know what they're here for, go ahead and decide your fate right now. But first, let's give a massive round of applause to our scriptwriting team, who has created a truly unique spin on an already fantastic story."

Tess and Cole stand to follow his directions while clapping along half-heartedly with the others, but I freeze at his declaration.

Because I suppose I should go along with them.

Spending the summer working on props or learning to

sew both sound like worthy pursuits, but I remain fixed, gaze locked on the stage.

What if instead of remaining in the background, I went for it? What if I spent the summer letting myself get a little lost in a character, exploring the part of myself I thought I was done with for good and bringing someone else to life?

It doesn't seem like a bad way to spend the time, even if it means I have to overcome the very reason why I quit acting in the first place.

I take a deep breath and sit back, letting myself adjust to this sense of purpose.

Joe continues clapping enthusiastically, long after the others have stopped. "This is going to be a summer to remember."

I think he's right about that.

FOUR

I sigh at the screen for what is surely the hundredth time.

My course descriptions are succinct, and while I appreciate brevity, rereading them over again doesn't exactly inspire joy. I rub my eyes to try and abate the dryness that is the direct result of my unblinking glare.

I have a college advisor overseeing my scheduling, and I've just opened three emails in a row with an excessive number of exclamation points. She's very congratulatory about how well I've done on the placement tests, which have tested me out of the remedial math and English courses.

Since I haven't declared a major, I'm still in mostly introductory classes such as Freshman Composition and U.S. History. Which is why in some ways, it just feels like another iteration of senior year—a much more expensive version, that is.

Thankfully, I'm only on the hook for room and board. My parents have some money set aside, but it's heavily supplemented by my savings account. Over the years, the very small amount of royalties from *Wanda* and the other projects accrued enough to give me some leeway, but it's not as much as I'd hoped to have as a cushion.

On top of the dread that surfaces while looking at this information, I also feel wildly guilty.

There are thousands—maybe millions—of people who would kill for this opportunity, and here I am spending an evening frowning at my computer. I'm definitely very grateful for the opportunity to attend at all, but as I continue to read through the summaries of what I'll be learning, I feel like I'm still selling myself on it.

College, to most people, feels like a natural progression from high school.

It's an idea I bought into a long time ago when teachers started spouting the ideal SAT scores and encouraging us to attend college fairs. All my friends and my ex-boyfriend, Lucas, were obsessed with getting logo sweatshirts of their dream schools and stalking campus maps.

But I've never come anywhere close to that level of interest or excitement.

The only thing that has inspired *anything* close to that in recent memory is the rush of being in the theater.

It's only been one day, but listening to Joe and the writers do a read-through of the script, commenting on inflections and making stage notes, enthralled me in a way nothing else has for as long as I can remember.

Sitting in the auditorium, even while watching minor adjustments to lighting and the curtain track, seems far more appealing than sitting in any classroom.

Maybe it's the combination of newness and nostalgia that's gotten into me tonight, but I'm weighed down.

And I want to float for a bit.

No, I think I *need* it.

Usually, I relegate myself to only one night a week of breaking and entering, but I'm hoping a quick dip in the pool will help me clear my mind.

I close my laptop and stretch my arms overhead. My neck and back muscles are stiff from the hunched-over position I've been fixed in for the past two hours.

I practically roll across the room to my dresser, then open the top drawer to eye the three bathing suits I own. My choices are a modest one-piece, my go-to black bikini, and then there's a fiery red number that's more straps than fabric.

They're just articles of clothing, but I'm trying to decide which one will help me get into the right mindset.

It's partly why costumes and fittings are so crucial to an actor's performance—it helps a person embody the character they need to play.

Even in my regular life, I've always been a little meticulous about what I wear for that reason. I want to *feel* the connection to what I wear.

I'm far from any sort of influencer or fashion icon, but I take care of my exterior, exaggerating my eyeliner when I'm exuding confidence or diving headfirst into my favorite oversized sweatshirt when I need the comfort.

What I wear is a reflection of who I am on the inside, which is why I'm stopped short, staring at the three options before me.

The one-piece seems juvenile and too stifling. The last

time I wore it was to a waterpark almost a year ago on a trip with Lucas and all the others who are merely a memory of my old life at this point. It was one last big hurrah before I moved and we subsequently grew apart.

And that little red bikini was a discounted impulse buy when we moved in and I saw the hole in the ground that would soon become the Kellers' pool.

At the time, I imagined I'd become friends with Tess—and many other people at my new school—but that never came to fruition. Aside from surface-level conversations in class, and a few partnered or group projects, my social life has been pretty much nonexistent.

I never became the girl next door or the girl in the red bikini, but I'm not so sure I'm at the point where I want to totally blend in, either.

I rub my eyes with the backs of my palms because this type of identity crisis is decidedly not what I need to pile on top of everything else.

Putting myself out of my misery, I quickly change into my trusted boring black bikini, then grab a towel and sneak downstairs.

The moon is super bright tonight, flanked by the dotted glow of stars. It's too late for me to be out here, given that we're closer to sunrise than sunset, but I don't back down.

I slip through the fence without difficulty, and just as my toes break through the surface, the back door opens.

Cole steps out wordlessly, then settles himself at the edge of the pool, just like he did the other night.

I focus on the movement of my limbs, letting the little ripples reach my collarbones. I'm a little surprised that the water doesn't betray any signs of my heart pounding in my chest. You'd think something fluttering so unabashedly would give outward signs, but I suppose that secret is well-contained in my chest cavity.

I glance at him, trying to decipher anything in his expression, but it's just dawned on me that he might have been waiting for me to appear here.

And that idea makes me jittery with delight.

Cole blows a pink bubble, then sucks it back in to crackle the air between his teeth. "I looked you up."

And all the warm, lovely feelings building inside me implode.

Out of all the things I expect him to say—make small talk, explain constellations, offer up his thoughts on the first day at the theater—this is not it.

I might be in his territory, swimming in his family's pool, but he's gone too far into mine. Him thinking about me based on our interactions is one thing, but the idea of him taking the time to cull up search results on me sends me into somewhat of an inner panic.

For all my prior reasoning of wanting to be my authentic self with Cole in this pool, this is not something I mentally prepared for.

The tickling feeling of mortification builds in my chest, and I try to breathe through it.

I move gently in the water, trying to breathe through the memories that flood my mind.

When I acted in front of cameras and small groups, it was enjoyable, almost easy. I memorized lines, stood where they told me to, and emoted under the assumption that I was a completely different person.

Commercials, too, were kind of interesting, with

shorter takes but the same amount of time spent dressing up in costumes and getting my makeup done.

Which is why Rachelle, my parents, and I didn't really think anything of the opportunity to present at a major award show. I got dolled up, memorized the words needed to announce the performer, and stood backstage.

I felt good, excited, and so many other emotions, but the moment I stepped out onto the stage, everything dissipated.

The light confidence was immediately replaced with outright horror as the bright lights hit my skin, bouncing off the sparkly pink dress I wore. The roaring applause continued as I unsteadily walked toward my mark.

My breathing sounded in my ears, and the sickening feeling of nausea and lightness hit me as I squinted toward the teleprompter.

I tried to ground myself by pretending there wasn't a packed theater of thousands of people while millions watched at home, but even I couldn't wish away my reality.

The pressure was immense, and my knees buckled.

Literally.

I fainted, faceplanted right on the middle of the stage, taking the microphone and my career down with me.

My memory is a little hazy from the rest of the night, but the news coverage in the hospital from the event replayed my fall twice before my mom turned it off.

I haven't searched my own name online in years, but from what others have shown me against my will, there are plenty of memes taken from stills of *Wanda,* along with the articles that describe me as a "failed child star" and the absolutely cringe-worthy sight of my passing out on live television.

I shudder at the thought.

It takes me a full minute to recover from this, and I have to channel all my emotions to steady myself, only to realize that he's been staring at me this entire time, waiting for a response.

I clear my throat, and the sound is weak. "Yeah?"

Casualness is what I'm going for, but I think my voice is a little strained.

I use the water to my advantage as I try to take control back over my mind and body, fanning out my arms and acting as if every droplet within my span is in my control.

"You're Wanda," he says. "You're *famous.*"

I want Cole to see me as I am now, not that girl all dolled up just to lose consciousness and everything she ever wanted. But that doesn't change the fact that he's armed with knowledge that I didn't give him.

"I was," I say carefully, forcing the evenness in my tone. "Once. It was a long time ago, though."

Cole doesn't buy my deflection. "No, you're on IMDb and everything. Why are you doing some stupid play when you've been on red carpets and stuff?"

And finally, my embarrassment shifts into something more powerful.

Anger.

Because it's not just some stupid play.

It's a life raft.

I blink at my own realization and how easily those words appear in the forefront of my mind. I *want* to try again, even if I've convinced myself it's just some little summer program.

"What are you doing here?" I retort, letting my annoyance show.

"Talking to you," Cole answers evenly.

"No, *here*." I gesture to our surroundings. "In this house. In this state. Why aren't you living some great, big, wonderful life in New York City? Why are you here, volunteering for a 'stupid' play?"

I swim closer to the wall, wanting to get a better view of his expression.

From this proximity, I can see the little changes, like the way his curious eyes narrow and somehow harden. I can't decide if he's processing my questions or has just decided not to answer me.

I tread water for a minute, waiting to see how he's going to respond, but he doesn't open his mouth.

And I decide if he's not going to give me anything, I'll be damned if I continue to entertain him.

I push off from the wall, sending little wakes in every direction as I kick my legs. I prepare to lose myself in my nightly practice, determined to do so before I shrivel up into a prune, regardless of my onlooker.

"You weren't out here last night," Cole says, voice somewhat quiet and contemplative.

I laugh in frustration, expelling the air from my lungs in choppy breaths. "You seem to be paying very close attention to me."

He shrugs in a way that signals he's totally unbothered, and I adopt that trait, too, merely taking him in as I bob in the water.

I can't help but compare him to Lucas, the only other boy I've ever really been interested in.

My ex-boyfriend was nice enough but almost painfully shy at times. He constantly overthought things, which is why the whole cheating thing is still such a shock. I thought I could read his every emotion and intention, but I guess no matter how long or how well you know someone, they can still do surprising and awful things.

Cole, by comparison, is clearly confident enough to commit light stalking and stare me down shamelessly.

And I very much enjoy it.

I need to understand more of him, his story, and his past. I want him to be honest with me, but I don't think it's going to be given easily.

"I'll answer one of your questions if you answer one of mine," I offer.

He quirks a brow. "Pretty cliché to play twenty questions, don't you think?"

"Is being cliché such a bad thing?" I pose as I swish from side to side. "Besides, who said anything about twenty?"

"Fine," he relents on an exhale.

I think I see the ghost of a smile, but it's hard to tell.

"But I get to go first," he adds.

"Okay," I agree, swimming back toward him. "What've you got?"

"Does Tess know you swim in her pool at night?" Cole asks lightly.

It's a softball question, so I don't hesitate to answer. "No. None of the Kellers do. Well, except you, and I don't think you're the type of person to rat me out."

"You're correct." Cole blows a tiny bubble, then sucks it back into his mouth.

I hang onto the wall and kick my feet out behind me. "Do you know how to swim?"

"Of course," he replies, eyeing the way I twist and turn.

With each passing second, I grow more comfortable in his presence.

Not because of anything he's doing but because every molecule of my body feels somehow unencumbered when I'm in the water.

That freedom, along with the attention his gaze lavishes on me, causes me to be a little jittery with excitement, but I think I'm hiding it well.

"Why aren't you living in LA or something?" Cole asks.

"I quit acting when I was a kid," I say automatically.

He runs a hand through his hair, tangling the ends slightly in his fingertips. "I know. I saw that you haven't done any projects lately. But still, you've got to give me more than that."

I fix my features to the pinnacle of innocence. "Do I?"

"Yes," he insists.

"Then I'll expect more in return from you." I chew on my bottom lip, surprised that I don't find it too terrible to let the words flow from my mouth. "I assume you saw it. The video of me passing out on stage?"

He nods. "Yeah."

"Well, after that happened, the big fancy studio that wanted to do a sequel of *Wanda* canceled the project. They were concerned that I didn't have 'what it took' to carry the film, and their decision had a rippling effect in the indus-try." I stop to let out a sigh. "But looking back, it was probably for the best. I hated being away from my friends, and I could tell all the travel and time apart was hard on my parents."

"Was it worth it?" Cole asks. "All the fame and fortune?"

I laugh. "If I had a fortune, I'm not sure if I'd be here. But also, that's two questions in a row."

"I'll make it up to you," he says.

I take a second to figure out how to articulate my response. "I'm not sure if it was worth it or how different my life could be if I stayed. I suppose I could have pushed through it, taken classes or different roles or something. But still, at the time, it seemed likely that even if it was what I wanted, I still might not have landed anything. But it's strange to think about what I possibly gave up."

I stop moving to look him in the eyes, watching him take in my words. I don't think it's active listening that causes him to nod—it's like he can relate.

"And now you're getting back into it?" Cole presses.

"I don't think so." I pause and consider. "Well, I'm not sure. Maybe not to that level. I don't know. I'm trying to enjoy it and take it slow."

"That's fair."

"Is it?" I tease. "Because you've asked me three questions in a row. It's my turn."

He sighs and waves his hand flippantly, like he doesn't care about what consequences may arise out of this agreement.

But I know I do.

"What are you doing here? Why did you make the sudden move? Did you leave…anyone behind?"

Part of me wants to sink under the water's surface in mortification at the questions that spill out, but I relax when I see the twitch at the corner of his lips, giving me the sense that I've amused him.

"That was a pretty roundabout way to ask me if I'm dating anyone," Cole says smartly. "It'd be pretty shitty of me to spend my nights out here with you, stargazing and bantering, if I did, wouldn't it?"

"You're supposed to be answering my questions," I remind him. "And with honesty, not ambiguity."

"No," he says forcefully. "I don't have a girlfriend."

"Well, why not?"

"Who knows."

"Of course you know," I argue.

"Why don't you have a boyfriend?" Cole counters.

"Who says I don't?"

"Tess."

I balk in surprise. "You asked her?"

"Yes," he says simply.

"Why?"

Cole crackles his gum in his teeth. "Because."

I huff at his one-word response. "Did they kick you out of New York because you infuriated anyone who tried to hold a conversation with you?"

I expect him to fire back an answer.

But he pauses, bringing a halt to our volleying rhetoric.

"No," he answers after a beat. "That's not why I left."

I intentionally soften my voice. "Well, then, why did you?"

His jaw moves in a steady rhythm as he chews. "I'm staying here for a while."

"But *why*?"

"Family business."

It's the most clipped response he's given me.

I take it as a signal that the fun is over, but just as I'm about to suggest my exit, he speaks again.

"My dad got into some trouble," Cole explains carefully. "He's in prison."

"Oh," I breathe.

His father is tied up, and his mother is in the past tense.

The thought makes me frown, not because I'm ashamed that I've taken advantage of the idea of parents as an infallible dual unit but because he doesn't have any.

It is a little odd that he's here with family he hasn't seen in years instead of friends or other relatives in New York, but then again, I don't exactly have the Keller family tree memorized. I only know the extended family as "the other Kellers" from Marlene's conversations in our kitchen.

Cole clears his throat. "So, what part are you auditioning for?"

My mind is still processing the very minimal but very interesting information he just shared. "What?"

"For the play," he adds. "You're going out for a role, right?"

"Yes," I say, allowing him to pivot the conversation in another direction. "I haven't decided yet. But, uh, maybe the Duchess?"

"I thought the character was a queen or something."

"It is," I confirm. "The Queen of Hearts is the main

villain in this story. Have you read the books or watched any of the movies?"

Cole shakes his head. "Nope."

"Well, I guess that doesn't matter. But it's a modern spin on the tale of a girl falling into a new world and being presented with decisions and challenges in each scene. It starts off the same, though, as the original book and the movie. Alice has to decide what adventure she's going to go on, and she has to choose if she's going to drink from a bottle or eat a piece of cake, which will transform her in different ways."

"Sounds like the beginning of *The Matrix*," Cole says, leaning back on his hands. "Red pill or blue pill."

"Never saw it," I admit.

His mouth drops open. "Never?"

I shake my head. "But in this story, Alice is led through a world of adventures, guided by the White Rabbit. Each time she meets a new character, a new obstacle is presented. Like, the Hatter speaking in riddles is kind of a play on a bad date. But she meets the other well-known figures, too, like the Duchess, the Dormouse, and the Caterpillar, which culminates in a face-off with the Queen of Hearts."

Cole, thankfully, doesn't appear to be bored by my long-winded explanation. "You're trying out for a background role?"

"It's not like I'm hiding," I defend. "I mean, the costume will probably be really cool, and I would have a few lines..."

"Interesting."

"What is?" I press.

He takes me in one more time. "That you think you're not the main character."

I'm still trying to decipher what exactly he's insinuating when the hallway light flickers on behind him.

I instantly recoil at the brightness, and Cole jumps up, illuminating his silhouette.

"I'll run interference," he says immediately, jogging back in the house.

I escape as quickly and quietly as I can, leaving a trail of watery footprints on the pavement.

Before I slip through the fence, I wonder if Alice felt this off-kilter when she stepped into a world she didn't think she would ever discover.

FIVE

The nervous energy isn't just coming from me, but I definitely carry my share.

I'm trying to hold it together, telling myself that we've all gathered here for a social call, but that internal lie combusts when Joe signals it's time to start the auditions.

Tess, Cole, and the other people who aren't auditioning shuffle out of the theater, which means with no one monitoring my shaking leg, I'm free to let it bounce as I chew on my thumbnail in the cover of darkness.

Joe sits beside his assistant and two writers in the front row. The group forms a panel, giving off serious singing competition vibes rather than a local community theater audition.

I've been out of the industry for years, but even I know there's an art to auditioning—trying to maneuver your own time on stage between people who are good but not great and those who aren't total disasters.

It's all about controlling the perspective around you and giving yourself a shot at being the best performance.

For that reason, I would never volunteer to go first, unless I had the utmost confidence in my ability, which is not something I've ever had, even as a kid.

Surprisingly, though, not even Esme raises her hand for an early turn.

She and her friends do make a point to laugh at all the newbies, though. It's clear that there are amateur actors in the ranks as early as the first few volunteers, and they mock them just loud enough that I can hear from two rows behind them.

One guy's hands shake so hard from nerves, I doubt he can even read the script.

Esme feeds off his mistakes like it fuels her own self-worth, but my heart breaks for him.

Watching that guy falter makes me even more nervous for my audition, so when Joe calls for everyone to break for lunch, I slip out of the theater to venture off alone with my script.

There's a little grassy area between the parking lot and the back door of the building that I take up residence on.

Esme and her friends pass by, chattering excitedly about getting takeout at a nearby chain.

I take a deep, reassuring breath, then pull out my copy of *In Wonder* and the brown bag lunch my mom shoved in my hands this morning.

I sink my teeth into my apple as I begin to read the opening stage directions, reviewing the little notes I scribbled in the margins yesterday.

I skim over some of the scenes, smiling slyly at the introduction of the White Rabbit. The guy who auditioned for that part this morning is absolutely going to get it, and I can't wait to see his full performance. He brought so much charisma and power to the role that he's a total shoo-in.

I only hope I can leave a fraction of the good impression I know he left on Joe.

Halfway through my peanut butter sandwich, I feel a looming presence beside me, interrupting my umpteenth read of the earmarked section of the audition material. I run my tongue along my teeth, ensuring there's no bread-crumbs stuck in them.

When I glance up, I expect and hope for Cole.

But I get Tess.

She sits beside me and adjusts a massive pair of sunglasses on the bridge of her nose, then helps herself to my blue corn chips without offering me a word.

I roll my eyes but don't comment, choosing to refocus on the words I'm attempting to memorize. It's not neces-sary for the audition, of course, but I'll feel better the more ingrained the material is in my mind.

I'm trying to put myself in the character's head, but I'm distracted by the sound of sniffling beside me.

I wish I had a tissue or something to offer because the sound of Tess—

"Are you crying?" Cole voices the question as the real-ization hits me.

He shoves his hands in his pockets and glances down at Tess with a look of disbelief.

I would think, being a part of the family, he would have

seen her display this emotion before, but he seems as stunned as I am.

I can't decide if he's more surprised by the little tears that trail down her face or at her decision to let them do so in such close proximity to other people.

"So?" Tess coughs out. "People cry."

"People do," Cole agrees. "But not you."

She snorts at that as she bats away the moisture.

"I don't think you shed one tear when you broke your arm when we were kids," he continues. "Or when we saw *The Lion King*, like some kind of sociopath. Even I cried when Mufasa died."

She manages a laugh. "Shut up, Cole."

"Are you okay?" I ask her as kindly as I can.

She removes her sunglasses, revealing her red-rimmed eyes, and presses her palms against her face. "Yes."

Cole sits down beside her, then reaches over to fish a few chips from the bag. "I can't imagine you're crying over the way I botched cutting those two-by-fours," he says lightly. "Even if you did tell Craig that it looked like he 'gave a child a handsaw.'"

"Well, in my defense, I was telling the truth," Tess says.

"Do you want to talk about it?" I ask tentatively.

She glares at me before she lets out a sigh. "I mean, not really."

"Oh, well—"

"It's Gabriela," Tess says suddenly, as if those words could no longer stay trapped inside her. "We…broke up last night."

I open and close my mouth a few times, unsure if she wants words of comfort or companionship.

The last time I saw the two of them together, they looked stupidly happy. I can picture their exact pose in their graduation robes before they spent the majority of the ceremony holding hands.

I wouldn't have put money on their breakup, given what I saw, but I suppose that was almost a month ago at this point.

"Oh," Cole breathes. "Why?"

She puts her sunglasses back on her face, like she's putting up a shield. "Do you want me to pry into *your* business?"

"Not really."

"Good," she says before holding up the empty bag of chips. "You got any more of these?"

I shake my head and offer her the other half of my sandwich.

Not just because I think she needs comfort—even if it's in the form of food—but I don't feel all that hungry right now anyway.

We settle into silence, with Tess eating my sandwich while staring off into space, Cole tapping out a beat on his knee, and me trying to focus on the script once again.

It goes on for a little while until Esme pulls back into the parking lot.

Music blares from her flashy red sports car as she zooms by us into a space, and my jaw drops open in astonishment as she steps out of the driver's seat.

Over our brief lunch break, she's gone from a normal teenager to the reincarnation of Alice herself.

Esme is decked out in a costume, complete with white

stockings, that famous light blue dress, and a black head-band that looks so chic and cute in her blonde hair.

I took care in crafting my own appearance this morning, donning a pale pink babydoll dress. At the time, I thought it looked kind of cute but regal enough to match my intended part, but now I just feel completely inadequate.

"What an asshole," Tess mutters, watching Esme sashay through the doors.

I stand immediately, assuming Esme's reappearance means it's time to head back inside. "Well, see you guys later," I offer lamely.

"Uh-huh," Tess says as I gather my garbage to take back with me.

She makes no move to join me, even though I'm pretty sure she's supposed to be helping backstage.

"Alexandra," Cole calls after I take a few steps.

I take a breath before I turn back. "Yeah?"

"Remember what I said."

"What'd you say?" Tess asks, gaze flicking between us.

He doesn't look at her when he answers, keeping his eyes locked on mine. "You're a main character," he says simply. "Allie in Wonderland."

Tess regards me with a tilted head. "I can see it."

"Thanks," I say, swallowing my surprise before heading back inside.

As I make my way to the wings to await my turn, Esme parades around onstage, halfway through Alice's monologue.

It's from a scene with Caterpillar and a train conductor. They're waiting for Alice to choose her next destination, and the whole situation signals a crossroads in her life.

Esme recites all the lines off-book, apparently having every single word memorized, and she floats through the scene with arrogance, channeling her own self-assurance into the part. Part of me is ready to believe she stomped right up on the stage and started speaking, expecting everyone to be ready for her.

When she finishes, she takes a bow, earning a few claps from those seated in the theater.

From my vantage point, I can see Joe's even expression as he simply nods and waves her offstage.

"Any volunteers to go next?" he calls, glancing around.

I wish I had some explanation for what propels me to step forward, but I don't. It's terrible timing, honestly, a move that goes against everything I know.

But my body acts of its own accord, completely disregarding the knowledge that I should wait to follow someone who won't outshine my own impression on those casting the play.

Esme is a shoo-in for the lead, and every single person here knows it.

She's one of three people going out for the role, and although she's not my favorite person or actor, she's got what it takes to carry the play.

Despite this knowledge, I realize something.

I want it.

Not because I think Esme is going to get it and I'm eager to build up some sort of rivalry with her.

I actually, *truly* hope to do this for myself.

I can't relate to the book or movie version of Alice, who naively stumbles along in her life, but I can see myself in this one. She's strong and determined, and although there are some setbacks and choices to be made, she's aware that her life is in her control.

She simply has to go for it.

And that's what I'm going to do.

"Alexandra Sutton," Joe calls in greeting.

I clear my throat and blink, trying to adjust to the warm lights in my vision. I dig my fingernails into my palm in an attempt to stay as in the moment as I can, not letting my past mishap interfere with my future.

"Hi," I say somewhat hoarsely.

"You'll have to thank your mother for me," he says conversationally. "My daughter is making a full recovery, and she loves the cast color."

"That's great," I tell him. "I'm glad to hear she's doing okay."

He smiles, then glances at the tablet in front of him. "You signed up to audition for the Duchess?"

"I did." I pause to smile. "I've changed my mind, though, if that's all right."

"Of course," he says, jotting down a note before smiling up at me. "What role do you think you're better suited for?"

"Alice."

I let that word settle between us, forcing myself not to look at Esme or listen to any of the murmuring.

He nods and sits back before waving a hand. "Please, go ahead when you're ready."

I should have taken the time to review this scene more deeply, but I'm oddly at peace with my spur-of-the-moment decision. I think I would have lost my resolve if this were premeditated.

I close my eyes briefly to channel the inner stillness I find late at night in the water, but instead of aiming for nothingness, I consider Alice.

She's lost in a world she doesn't feel like is her own, but she has choices to make, and Caterpillar, smoking from a pipe, demands an answer. I can smell the tobacco burning and mixing in with the fresh air as I envision him tempting me.

I step forward, into the full spotlight, then I begin.

"I'm at a crossroads, but I will not fall to your temptations, Caterpillar," I say forcefully. "I don't need your beautiful words or false promises or insinuations of who I am. I didn't ask for your thoughts on where to go from here, and I don't want them."

As if I am shedding his influence, I straighten my posture and raise my chin.

"I may look small and unusual to you," I continue. "But I am strong and fierce, and I will not tolerate your cunning phrases and misdirection any longer."

I back away, just as the stage directions instruct, putting distance between myself and the imaginary set I've constructed in my mind.

"And if we cross paths again, I shall not be as polite or gentle or kind as I am in this moment, and you'll do well to remember that."

My chest heaves from emotion, and I stop suddenly, blinking as a round of hearty applause fills my ears.

Unlike Esme, I poured my soul into those words, and I can't simply snap out of the performance and offer a bow.

But I do come out of myself enough to see that I've earned a wide grin of approval from Joe.

I turn quickly, intending to decompress in the darkness backstage, but as I step out of the spotlight, I see Cole's smirk in the audience.

It's at that moment I know that even if I don't get the role, I've tapped into a part of myself I've long forgotten.

SIX

I imagine Joe and the others are locked in a room somewhere.

Possibly with corkboards covered in cutout pictures and strings running faces to pages of notes and diagrams—and whatever else is usually included in those crime scene shows.

Casting an entire play seems like a daunting task to me, but I suppose that's the role they've signed up and prepared for, so they're up to the challenge.

Because the truth is that although a person can have a great audition, there's a cohesion needed with the other characters, too.

It's why in film work, chemistry tests exist. I don't think there's a stage equivalent to that, but I'm honestly not sure if it's more important on screen or on stage. Regardless, I've been running through a bunch of scenarios in my mind, trying to fit the actors to the roles and create cohesion.

The puzzle of casting keeps my mind occupied as I unload nearly a dozen paint buckets from the back of a pickup truck.

"Arms already dead?" Andrew teases.

He's the guy who absolutely crushed the White Rabbit role, and while I was excessively complimentary when we introduced ourselves originally, he was even more so about me as Alice.

"A little bit," I admit, shaking out my limbs. "I didn't realize that being an actor required this type of manual labor."

He takes one of the buckets from me, then places it on the table with the others. "They'll have to take out your sleeves to accommodate Alice's bulging biceps if you keep this up."

"Don't jinx it," I warn him.

"The character or the muscle building?"

I laugh. "Both."

Andrew grins at me. He has one of those obnoxiously white smiles that I have no choice but to return, and it's effortless to do so.

I'm grateful he and I have formed an easy friendship over these past few days.

As Joe and the team play casting Jenga, every single potential cast member has been assigned to help with set and props. It's a smart way to get all hands helping before the roles are announced and rehearsal officially kicks off next week.

Most of us have been relegated to hauling items around in the hot sun.

Not Esme, of course—she and her loyal followers are

tasked with reorganizing the makeup and hair closet in the protection of air conditioning.

This heat actually makes me want to go swimming in the daylight, just to cool off.

"A few of us are going out tonight," Andrew tells me as he tears open the packaging for a variety of paintbrushes.

"Oh?" I don't return his eagerness as I focus on organizing them by size.

"Do you want to join us?"

I shift on my feet. "What are the plans?"

"Uh, we're grabbing dinner," he says, temporarily fanning himself with a piece of cardboard. "Then maybe bowling after?"

"Oh, absolutely not," I reply immediately.

He chuckles. "You embarrassed that someone might show you up?"

"It's the shoe thing. Not only are they hideous and uncomfortable but they've been worn by god knows how many people."

"They clean them," he says as if that somehow cancels out hundreds of sweaty feet in clown shoes.

I shudder. "I've been talked into it once before, and I'll never do it again."

"Fine, fine," Andrew relents. "Next time, I'll try to get the activity pre-approved by you."

"Thank you," I say with a smile.

"I'm not as picky, though. As long as there's cold air, I'll do almost anything right now. This is torture."

I groan and toss my hair up in a pile on top of my head. "I know."

But the truth is, temperature aside, I don't mind it all that much.

Not only do I get some much-needed vitamin D but I've been able to watch Cole work whenever I please. And I've done so often enough that Andrew called me out on it within an hour of us working together.

It's only been one full week of the program, but Cole seems to have really gotten into the groove with his role. From what I can tell, he's assimilating nicely among the crew. I've also noticed a few times when he's happily getting pointers from Craig, who is in charge of set production and owns a custom woodshop across town.

Across the way, Cole tugs at the hem of his shirt in an attempt to cool himself, giving me a generous view of his abs.

I gawk openly at the sight until Andrew nudges me with his elbow.

"Earth to Alexandra," he teases.

"Sorry," I say, cheeks reddening as I focus my attention. "What were you saying?"

"I was asking what else you have planned for this weekend. You know, aside from refreshing your inbox to see if the cast list has arrived yet."

Andrew and I make small talk the rest of the day, sharing stories about school and theater experience to distract ourselves from the sun and heat, until Joe pulls us all back into the theater, congratulating us on a great first official week.

On the way home, Tess tries to distract herself from the harrows of her breakup by cranking up both the air conditioning and the stereo volume.

It's a good way to decompress from the week, music up and pedal pressed to the floor.

At a stoplight, I pull the strap of my dress aside on my shoulder to check my tan line, and I'm surprised how defined it is after today. As I turn my eyes back toward the road, I catch Cole's gaze in the rearview mirror, and he smirks.

I barely suppress my smile as we part ways in the driveway.

Then I spend the entire night thinking about that little moment before succumbing to a deep sleep where I dream that I'm falling through a rabbit hole.

———

"You got it!" My mother screams in delight.

I turn the phone to my dad to reveal the full cast list, showing him that I've received top billing.

"Allie is Alice," my dad says excitedly. "This is fantastic news."

They both jump up and hug me, speaking over top of each other to tell me how proud they are. It's a good feeling all around—the actual landing of the role as well as the complete buy-in and support from them.

"We need to celebrate," my dad declares.

Mom nods in agreement. "Of course."

When I brought home straight As last fall, we marked that achievement with frozen yogurt, which is apparently a healthier alternative to ice cream.

But it tasted like sour milk to me.

"What about lunch at the Green Grille?"

"Oh, no, that's okay," I protest immediately, recalling how much kale is on that menu. "The hugs are enough."

"Nonsense," my mom insists. "If we head out right now, we can get the brunch appetizer sampler to start."

I grimace. "It's really—"

My dad appears to pick up on the reason why I'm hesitating. "How about we let Allie decide the place?"

My mom blinks in confusion. "I thought you liked that spinach chicken wrap you had last time?"

"It was…fine," I bite out.

"But I recreated it for dinner for *weeks*," she says, a little annoyed.

"I know, but you were so excited about it. I just didn't want to ruin it for you."

She stares at me, equal parts hurt at the lie and annoyed at all the effort she put into it, and I feel awful for both reasons.

"Allie, just tell us where you want to go," my dad presses.

I hesitate, not wanting to contribute to the tense vibe of the room.

My mom sighs. "What about—"

"It's Allie's celebration," he interrupts. "*She* should choose."

"Fine," she snaps at him, then turns to me. "Wherever you want."

They both stare me down, waiting for my decision, so I relent. "Well, I often heard kids at school talking about some diner called Mickey's not too far from here."

My mom wrinkles her nose. "Oh, that's right by the hospital. It's pretty much all grease and fried—"

"Perfect," my dad says with a note of finality. "Let's head out."

It's not exactly a celebratory mood in the car. They keep their eyes forward and out the front windshield, and it's completely silent. I would almost prefer Tess's company to theirs at this moment, and that realization makes me groan internally.

I want to channel my inner Cole and crank up some rock music, but my parents pretty much listen to NPR or nothing.

Instead, I'm stuck running our conversation through my head over and over, picking out the ways I could have diffused the situation or gotten out of it altogether.

I crane my neck in an attempt to get a glimpse of any signs of life coming from the Keller house, but there are none. I do, however, notice that Marlene's car isn't in its usual place in the driveway.

"Does Marlene have a shift this morning?" I ask, hoping to cut through the tension.

"What?" It takes a second for my mother to register the question. "Oh. No, I don't think so. Unless she picked one up."

I let out a sigh. "Look, Mom, I'm really sorry for not telling you about the spinach thing."

"It's just a few meals," my dad says, waving off my apology on her behalf.

She turns to him with fire in her eyes. "*Just* a few meals? That I meticulously prepared while dead on my feet from taking care of people all day and night at the hospital? Only to learn months later that it was all for nothing?"

My dad is silent for a beat, then his tone shifts from bravado to apologetic. "I guess not."

"It's fine," she snaps before turning to look out the window.

No one says a word until we're seated at a booth with well-worn leather cushions, and it's the server who helps my parents snap out of this quiet standoff.

They put in orders for breakfast specials—eggs, toast, turkey bacon, and a side of fruit—while I order up a massive platter of chocolate chip pancakes.

I fiddle with the straw wrapper while watching the other families around us smile and laugh.

Usually, we're one of them.

"Is everything okay?" I ask curiously.

"Yes," Mom and Dad say in unison.

I give them my most skeptical look. "Maybe this was a bad idea."

My mom shakes her head. "Your dad was right. We're here to celebrate all your achievements, Allie."

"We're so proud of you," my dad says, plastering a big smile on his face. "We've known you're a star your entire life. We're so proud to see you returning to something you're so good at."

This injection of happiness and praises, whether it's genuine or not, doesn't make me feel as expected.

"Thanks," I reply before taking a sip of my water.

"You know, if Joe Morales opens up a fall program, you could always try out if your fall schedule allows," my mom says. "But I understand if you want to have the full college experience without it."

"Such a shame the university doesn't offer a theater program," my dad laments.

"Well, had we known she was going to be interested in it a year ago, maybe you would have taken that job in Philadelphia instead."

My dad shrugs. "Too late now."

She scoffs. "It's never too late."

"Do you even want to get back into the industry?" My dad asks the question but doesn't wait for my response. "I'm sure Rachelle would be delighted to hear it if that's the case. Not to mention some of those connections we made with other actors and producers years ago."

"Or," my mom interjects, "you could start with theater, get some press interest, then perhaps start reviewing manuscripts to see if anything in film or television appeals to you. Taking it nice and slow."

"She's been moving slow ever since she turned down the *Wanda* sequel," my dad says. "If she's serious about this, she needs to jump back in as quickly as she can."

They continue bickering back and forth, not even bothering to wait for my opinion.

It's a strange feeling to be on the outside, but as I listen to them continue on, I'm unsure if they're actually arguing about me or if they just want something to argue about.

I feel like I'm caught in between them, and it's not exactly comforting.

"Here you are!"

The server is a cheerful and oblivious interruption.

Usually I get secondhand nervousness when waitstaff at restaurants balance more than two plates at once, but I've never been so grateful for the three of us to all get served at once.

I cut into my sweet, fluffy goodness with the side of my fork.

Because even if everything about this situation sucks right now, at least I have a massive stack of carbs, butter, and chocolate.

It looks *way* better than what my parents ordered.

"So, you should hear from the university soon to find out who your roommate is," my dad says after a few bites.

"Yes," I say evenly. "That's what my advisor said, too."

"I hope you have better luck than I did my freshman year," he tells me with a chuckle before steering us down memory lane.

My mom immediately tunes him out as he begins to tell a story about the time his roommate convinced him to go to some rave in a frat basement. The punchline is that they both landed in the hospital with alcohol poisoning, and I already know that it's definitely not going to be a part of my college bucket list.

I smile tightly as he continues on, wishing this whole thing didn't feel so off.

My parents rarely argue, and when they do, it's usually resolved before I even fully understand what they disagreed on.

But the tension between them right now is making me lose my appetite, which is a massive disappointment, given the amount of beautiful, half-melted chocolate chips before me.

"Do you *have* to eat your eggs like that?" my mom asks,

interrupting my dad as he uses his toast to soak up the runny yolk.

He sighs and shakes his head. "Now you have a problem with my breakfast?"

"I'm gonna go to the bathroom," I announce, dropping my napkin on the table and scooting out of the booth.

I hope the few minutes I plan to hide in the bathroom will give my parents time to get on the same page—or whatever it is they need—so I can eat my pancakes in peace.

As I wash my hands, just for something to do while I'm in here, a girl emerges from the stalls.

I catch a look at her in the large mirror reflected before us, and she steps up to use the faucet beside mine. There's something familiar about her shiny, black hair and eyebrow piercing.

After staring at her far too long, it finally hits me.

I flick the excess water from my hands into the sink and reach for a paper towel. "Gabriela, right?"

She glances up and narrows her eyes in appraisal. "Yeah?"

"I'm Alexandra," I remind her. "Tess's neighbor."

But then I realize there's absolutely no reason she should know who I am.

We didn't have classes together during the one year we attended the same school, and I only know who she is because I stared out my bedroom window on the rare occasions she and Tess hung out by the pool.

I'm embarrassed by how stalkerish that sounds.

"Okay," Gabriela says dismissively.

I can't even feign arrogance, like Cole seems to do so

expertly, and in no way is this situation and conversation with Gabriela cute or redeemable enough to play off.

So I cringe and move to get the hell out of this bathroom, resigned to my fate of going from one awkward situation to the next.

"Hey," she says, stopping me before I leave.

I look at her over my shoulder. "Yeah?"

"What has Tess been saying about me?" Somehow her question comes across as hard and vulnerable at the same time. "Did she tell anyone what happened?"

"Oh, uh, no," I answer quickly. "Only that you broke up."

She fixes her face back into an emotionless mask. "Good."

Her reaction makes me more curious than ever, but it is absolutely not my story to know. I mean, I definitely wouldn't want Tess to pry into my personal business, so I head back to the table.

My parents, thankfully, have resumed a shred of normalcy in my absence, sharing bites from each other's plates as they make small talk.

I spend the remainder of the meal spearing chocolate chips with my fork, counting down the hours until I can float and let this all go.

SEVEN

I sneak out later than I usually do.

My dad passed out on the couch, and I had to make sure he was dead asleep before I snuck out, in fear of having to explain myself to him.

As a consequence, or maybe it's a benefit, I stay in the water far longer than normal. I get to stare for hours at the constellations and watch the darkness abate slowly. The early signs of the sunrise flood the sky as I finally resign to pull myself out.

I try to tell myself that I'm just appreciating the scenery and that it has absolutely nothing to do with Cole not appearing.

But I admit my disappointment quietly to myself as my head hits my pillow.

I'm a little ashamed that I spend most of Sunday staring out my bedroom window, glancing up repeatedly as I paint my nails a shiny purple color.

The three other Kellers take shifts doing yard work, and Cole doesn't join them.

As curious as I am about the disappearing act, I don't want to be the type of girl who just sits around and pines after a guy she barely knows.

Absolutely not.

I have an entire play to memorize and a wayward Alice to channel, and that's what I fixate on for my waking hours until the next morning when it's time to head to the theater.

By the time I turn on the air conditioning in my car and wait for the Kellers to slide in, I'm feeling good about the coming week.

I'm going to show up to rehearsal, kick ass in my role, be off-book within days, and it's going to be so—

"Where's Cole?"

I ask the words within a second of the passenger door opening, finding Tess alone and scowling.

"I don't know," she says as she slams the door shut.

"You don't know?" I repeat.

She shrugs and kicks her feet up, putting her sandals directly on the glove box.

I give her a look of disbelief, then shift the car into drive. "You don't have any idea at all?"

"Who's asking?" Tess snaps.

"Me." I withhold an eyeroll. "The person who chauffeurs you both every single day."

Tess sighs as she inspects her cuticles. "He's back in New York."

"Back?" I repeat. "Like, permanently?"

"Something came up with his dad. I don't know what, nor do I care enough to hear about the drama from that side of the family. I have enough to worry about on my own."

I grimace as I tap the steering wheel. "About that."

"About what?"

I totally forgot about my run-in with Tess's ex-girlfriend until this moment, and I feel compelled to come clean about it.

"I saw Gabriela the other day," I say, glancing at her quickly as we cruise along.

Tess sits up and gives me her full attention. "What? Where? What'd she say? Tell me everything."

This panicky behavior is something I've never witnessed in her before, so I try to assuage her quickly.

"Bathroom at Mickey's. I said hello, and she wanted to know if *you* had said anything to me about her."

"What did you say?" Tess demands.

I hold up both hands as we hit a stoplight, like I'm trying to show my innocence. "That you only said that you broke up."

"Good," she breathes, sinking back into the passenger seat. "Good, good, good."

And for once, Tess becomes the one who is lost in thought and fidgeting.

I now realize it's not exactly comforting behavior, but I don't comment on it.

She jumps out of the car immediately when I come to a stop in the parking lot, and I let her go on ahead of me without protest.

All the unanswered questions regarding the Keller

family are giving me a headache, and I rub my temples as I step into the theater.

I jump back in surprise as I'm met with a crowd of happy—for the most part—cast and crew. I'm caught up in a tizzy of congratulatory hugs from people I haven't met yet, and I'm very grateful for it all.

"Alexandra," Joe calls from the stage.

"Hi," I say back, a little shyly.

He holds his hands in a sweeping grand gesture as he stands before a few arranged tables and chairs. "Our Alice."

Although a part of me desperately wants to, I don't falter under the stare of every single person in the room.

Instead, I channel the pride I feel for landing the role, holding my chin high as I climb the stairs and take the seat marked for me. After I sit, I quickly scan the room, taking in the vacancies around the table.

I catch Esme's glare from her seat, noting she's pushed aside her "QUEEN OF HEARTS" placard, before I continue on.

The man who was ridiculously nervous to audition appears to have landed a small speaking role as Dormouse, who Alice accidentally insults at the beginning of the play. The part fits him well because even if he can't control his nerves, I think his shaking will lend credibility.

"Am I late?" Andrew asks, taking the seat beside me. "For a very important date?"

"I think we're still waiting for a few more people," I say. "But congratulations, White Rabbit. I was right."

"*I* was right," he returns. "You're going to be an ass-kicking Alice."

"I hope so."

Andrew's eyes widen briefly over my head, so I turn to take in the gaze of the person who landed the role of the Hatter.

"I'm Beau."

"Alexandra," I say brightly. "It's nice to meet you."

"It's nice to meet *you*. I loved *Wanda* growing up. I had posters on my walls and made my mom put a DVD player in my room so I could watch it." Beau pauses and smiles sheepishly before sitting down. "But, like, in a totally normal and healthy way of admiration."

I smile again, though I doubt it looks genuine, and redirect the conversation. "Have you met Andrew, the White Rabbit?"

"Hey," Andrew says in greeting. "Nice to meet you, man."

Beau leans over to shake his hand and smiles. "You too. But I'm actually non-binary."

"So sorry," Andrew apologizes quickly. "They/them pronouns?"

"No worries, and yeah." Beau runs their fingers through the bright blue tendrils hanging on their forehead. "Please tell me I'm not the only one doing this program for the first time."

"It's a first for me," I admit with a reassuring smile. "But Andrew's an old pro."

"I grew up not too far from here, so this is actually my sixth summer," Andrew tells us. "This is the biggest role I've landed to date, though, so I'm really excited."

"I didn't know that." I smile at him again, then turn to Beau. "What made you join? Are you studying theater?"

"Oh, I wish. But my parents would die. They have a

hard enough time coping with this hair color and my decision to go to school out of state, so it's a nice, stable major of software engineering for me."

"Mostly the same for me," Andrew says. "Except I'm a business major."

"Oof," Beau breathes. "Have you had to take macroeconomics yet?"

Andrew manages to groan and laugh at the same time. "Totally brutal."

"All right, everyone, let's get started," Joe announces, calling everyone to attention. "I want to try to do at least one full read-through before lunch, so let's get to it."

And so we do.

I've read the script probably a dozen times now, but there's something magical about hearing all the different voices.

Joe reads the stage directions, pushing us along nicely, and even though we're merely sitting *on* the stage and not moving across it, the whole thing feels more real.

Some of the lines we're reading are pulled directly from the book originally written in the 1800s, but most of the dialogue is new. They cut a few characters and condensed others to simplify the plot, and in their place, the writers added social commentary along with a few jokes.

Andrew murmurs little comments to me, and I relax more and more as we go along, despite being under the scrutiny of certain others.

It takes me a while to realize that I'm having *fun*, which isn't something I can ever recall experiencing in my former acting life.

"Great work, everyone," Joe praises as we break for

lunch. "Now that we've gotten through it once, be ready for my nitpicking to begin."

There's a roll of laughter as the cast files out.

I find it a little difficult to leave the stage when I've been having such a serene experience, so different to the one I've associated with it for years, so I stay behind.

In solitude, I shamelessly inhale the scent of fresh paint that emanates from the quickly accumulating props.

I spin around, taking it all in, but as I come to a stop, my stomach grumbles loud enough that I'm certain if anyone were sitting in the actual theater, they would have heard it.

I open my purse and frown, realizing I left my lunch sitting in the car. My peanut butter sandwich has likely melted into something barely palatable. But it's all I brought with me, so I should at least go investigate its condition.

As I take a shortcut from backstage to the parking lot, I'm stopped in my tracks by the sound of arguing.

"I'm only staying on out of respect for you, Joe," Esme growls. "But you have to admit this is ridiculous."

I peek around the corner, taking in her aggressive stance and Joe's somewhat defensive posture.

He holds his hands up in an appeasing gesture. "Esme, come on, you know it's not—"

"Personal?" she sputters in disbelief. "Joe, you made promises to me. You spent all spring telling my parents that picking this production instead of that one in Los Angeles would be great for me."

"It will be," he says reassuringly. "I said it then, and it's still true now. My program is what's best for you."

She rolls her eyes.

I see the flash of irritation on his features before he snaps. "Perhaps it's not your acting ability but your respect and humility that needs brushing up on."

Esme laughs, but it sounds more like a cackle to my ears. "How are those things going to get me in front of all your industry friends?"

"I've already dropped your name to several of them, and they're eager to meet you. They'll be here for the performance, and they'll be impressed by your work and stage presence. At least, they will be if you can keep your ego in check long enough to say your lines."

"But Alexandra as Alice? Come on, she hasn't even—" Esme brings her thought to an abrupt stop.

I hide myself further in the shadows backstage, preparing to duck behind a few stacked boxes if I need to.

"That's it, isn't it?" she says, slightly stunned. "You're using Alexandra's stupid childhood stardom to get more attention for this production."

"No," Joe says immediately. "Absolutely not. She earned that role."

"But with the theater on the brink of closing, isn't it a great idea to leak her involvement to the press?" Esme sneers, "Innovative way to sell tickets, huh? Capitalizing on her name while making all these bullshit promises to me."

"Jesus Christ, Esme," Joe says on an exhale. "They say actors are dramatic, but this is absurd."

"You're telling me the thought never crossed your mind, then?" Esme presses. "That she'd get more attention for your little theater program."

"Well, I didn't say that," Joe admits.

I let out a sigh, hating myself for being glued to every word.

"Exactly," Esme snaps.

"Her audition blew yours out of the water," Joe says slowly. "And that's the only thing you need to worry about, Esme. Your own performance. How are *you* going to do better?"

And seeing that I've been a part of a lot of conflict, here and at home, I wonder if I should be asking myself the same question.

EIGHT

"Well, that was one hell of a first week," Andrew says as we walk toward the parking lot. "Long but good, I guess."

"Understatement," I retort.

The first five days of rehearsal were productive, but I didn't account for how draining these long days of reading the same material over again would get.

My brain feels like mush, and my feet feel like lead, even though we haven't started blocking out our scenes yet.

I suppose going from weeks of sleeping in and enjoying a lazy summer to an expedited theater program is going to be an adjustment.

But all things considered, even though I feel weighed down physically, my heart and soul feel light and fulfilled.

"On the bright side," I continue, playing up my cheerfulness. "I think we've had enough read-throughs that I have everything memorized."

He chuckles and kicks an errant stone across the pavement. "By the end of this, we'll probably be able to switch roles without anyone noticing."

"I don't know about that. I mean, I overheard the costume department discussing whether the White Rabbit should wear a top hat, which I'm sure you'd look way better in than me."

"Obviously." Andrew grins. "But next week should be better."

"Definitely. I'm looking forward to starting to *move* while we rehearse. And the staggered rehearsal schedule should give the other cast members a few breaks."

He lets out an exaggerated sigh. "Such a shame we are both so awesome that we have to basically be in every single scene."

I laugh and shake my head. "Andrew."

"What? It's true, and you know it." He twirls his keys on his finger. "No harm in being our own biggest supporters."

As we approach my car, I smile at him. "Well, I think I'm going to go home and crash."

"Me too," he says through a yawn. "Although, Beau asked if I wanted to get lunch and run lines with them on Sunday, so I might do that. We only live a few streets apart, apparently."

"That's great," I say as I open the door to my Jeep. "I, on the other hand, am absolutely not picking up the script even once this weekend."

Andrew snorts as he continues toward his own car. "I'll see you on Monday?"

"Yeah. See you!"

I idle in my car, waiting around for Tess, only to recall

she mentioned she was going out with some of the back-stage crew after today's rehearsal.

Annoyed at myself for delaying my rest that much longer, I blast my music and my air conditioning, pointing all the cold air vents in my direction.

I'm drained, completely exhausted, but it somehow feels satisfying.

When I arrive home, I don't get to dive face-first onto my bed, though, because my mom wants to chat me up about my fall classes. And after the whole debacle with the celebratory lunch, I've been treading lightly around both my parents.

Finally, sweet relief comes when she gets a work phone call, and I shuffle up toward my room. No matter how tired I am, I always take the time to go through my skin care routine, and once I'm all moisturized and comfortable in my pajamas, I pass out.

Most of Saturday is spent in recovery mode, but I also count down the hours until my parents, Marlene, and Mr. Keller head out. It's not so much their leaving that I'm anticipating as much as their tipsy arrival back home.

I watch their arrival through my bedroom window, then give them an hour to pass out before I make my move.

I've been in Alice's head since I landed the role, pushing down my own feelings to give everything I can to the character, so I'm looking forward to the feeling of weightlessness that my weekly ritual brings.

Out of habit, I reach for my black bathing suit, but I stop short just as my fingertips land on the fabric.

I've really pushed myself this week, proving that I can and should be the main character of a story.

So why am I so content on blending in? Even while just on my own?

I smile as I slide on the red bikini.

The straps are a little more complex than I'm used to, so I have to use the mirror to ensure I've done the neck and back straps correctly.

Once satisfied, I turn and study my reflection, and I'm invigorated by this one small, yet bold, decision.

I feel like I'm being rebellious, even though I'm only going to spend an hour or two by myself under the stars. At least, that's what I thought I was in for, but after I make my way through the fence, I stop short.

Instead of sitting on the edge of the concrete, Cole is perched up on one of the middle steps, half-submerged in the water.

The serenity he exudes as he glances up at the stars is so captivating that at first I don't even notice he's shirtless. When I do, my eyes bug out of my head, and I gasp as I process the lines of his muscles and tight abdomen.

"Where have you been?" I sputter out.

He glances up as I step toward him, and when he takes in my presence, his face somehow darkens even as his eyes light up.

"New York," he murmurs, gaze slowly moving down my body.

I hold myself proudly, not cowering under his attention.

This is the most uncovered I've been in someone else's presence since my breakup with Lucas, and I honestly forgot what it feels like to have someone appraise me this way.

I recognize the interest and lust in his features, but instead of feeling nervous, it makes me feel powerful.

Slowly, I settle down on the step beside him, still conscious of his eyes on me.

Cole shifts, turning toward me slightly, and his thigh grazes mine.

The skin-to-skin contact makes my insides feel like they're on fire, despite the pool's temperature, but outwardly I remain cool and indifferent.

"Did you have a nice trip?" I ask nonchalantly as ripples run across the water.

Because, really, there's no reason I should care about his sudden disappearance.

I barely know him, and other than our shared time in the car and the two other times we've done this, we don't interact. We're not friends, regardless of being in close proximity, so he had no obligation to give me a heads-up that he was going to run along to a different state.

But still, the rational part of my brain refuses to ignore the connection between us.

We haven't touched or even really opened up to each other, but I'm drawn to him.

It's more than attraction, I know that.

Or maybe it's just on a level I have yet to experience.

Never in my life have I felt such a need to be in someone's presence or watch how they move and interact with other people, trying to determine if it's different than the way he treats me.

"It wasn't really..." Cole trails off, then frowns. "Tess didn't tell you?"

I kick my feet out, letting my legs drift as I sit back, resting my elbows on the step behind me. "Nope."

No one tells me anything.

And I'm starting to not be okay with it.

Cole wrings his hands, having some sort of inner debate. "My dad is Garrett Keller."

"Okay?"

He sits silent, seemingly waiting for some sort of recognition to hit me.

When it doesn't, he adds, "The CFO of Ellison Incorporated...the company that's basically burning down to the ground with all their bad financial dealings and working violations?"

I don't exactly understand the meaning of all those words and what they imply, but I can feel the weight of the seriousness of the situation.

It doesn't mean I know what to say, though.

"Oh."

"Yeah." He rubs the back of his neck with his hand. "I guess it's not big news here, but in New York, it's a major topic of conversation. And not just with my friends and stuff. It's kind of weird to see my father's face plastered on the covers of tabloids."

"So, that's why you're really here," I guess.

"Yes," he admits quietly. "He's in prison, being held without bail."

The pieces are starting to come together. "And did something happen? That made you go back?"

"The trial started last week. I didn't even want to go, but his legal team said my presence would be good for him. And I thought it would. I mean, he is shitty, but he is my *father.*" He pauses and shakes his head. "It wasn't until I was accosted by reporters outside the courtroom that I realized he didn't want me there for moral support but to make him look good in the press."

I wince. "I'm sorry."

"You shouldn't feel sorry for me," Cole says earnestly.

"Why not?" I tuck my hair behind my ears, wanting him to see an unobstructed view of my sincerity. "This is a crappy situation."

"People have actual problems in this world, and I'm just some stuck-up rich kid whose dad got caught doing bad things."

"You didn't sign up for all this," I argue.

"But I benefited from it. I mean, when it all went down last spring, I didn't even think about the workers he ripped off or the families who couldn't afford rent or groceries. I was more concerned about the fact that I wouldn't get to travel around Europe this summer with my friends like I planned. Or go to Yale in the coming term since they revoked my admission."

I blink. "You got into *Yale?*"

"Yeah," he says glumly. "But now it looks like I'm stuck here, in my aunt and uncle's basement, until I turn eighteen and figure out what the hell I'm going to do next."

While it's difficult for me to relate to exactly what he's going through, I can understand some of it.

It seems like his entire world turned upside down in such a short time.

And if I learned anything about my time in the public eye, it's that complete strangers are the biggest critics and can inflict the most pain.

There's another layer to that in his case, though, because I got to escape the industry and go back to normal life, but every comfort Cole knew is unavailable now.

My heart aches for how lonely he must feel.

"Well, I'm glad you're here," I say honestly.

He raises an eyebrow. "Yeah?"

I exhale thoughtfully. "I know it's not ideal, but escaping New York and getting some distance from that pressure will take the burden off of you for a little while. It's like when I spent time in LA as a kid. Everyone knew who I was and followed me with cameras, and it was really overwhelming. But when I went back home to my friends, everything was back to normal. So maybe it's good that you're getting a change of perspective this summer."

"Maybe," he allows.

It's clear by that response that my simple reassurance isn't going to be enough.

"And if that doesn't make you feel better, I have something else we can try," I offer.

His forehead creases and he regards me somewhat tentatively. "What's that?"

"Let's play pretend," I say, slowly wading into the water. "It's kind of an actor thing that I've always done. Or it might just be a *me* thing, but I think it will help."

"Is that what you do when you float?"

"Not usually, but we're going to do it now," I insist, beckoning him to join me. "It seems like a shame to be sitting at the edge of the pool and not going all the way in. Come on."

Despite his reluctant attitude, he follows me in immediately, nearly closing the distance between us.

It feels romantic, even intimate, to have him in here with me with our exposed skin and the water blanketing us together. But I'm all business at this moment, knowing that he needs distraction, not my quiet lusting for him.

I alternate between swimming and bouncing on my toes while Cole simply walks, having no problem in the water's depth.

"Okay, how does this work?" he asks, indulging me.

"You have to imagine a scenario and put yourself in it," I say as I bob up and down. "Like, if you could be anywhere right now, where would you be?"

He sways where he stands, and I take it as a sign that he's slowly becoming less rigid.

"I don't even know, honestly," he says after a minute of silence.

"How about Tahiti?" I suggest.

"Tahiti? You've been?"

I laugh. "Definitely not. I've never even left the country."

"Really?"

"But that doesn't matter," I insist, smiling wryly. "Because we're not Cole and Alexandra right now. We're two swim instructors preparing lessons for our elder beginner swimmers."

"Elder beginner swimmers?" Cole parrots with a chuckle.

"It could be a thing," I say dismissively. "Last week, we got them to tread water and doggy paddle, but they're ready to learn an actual stroke. What do you think we should start with?"

Cole considers it for a beat. "Backstroke."

"Why's that?"

"It's the easiest transition for people who are nervous about putting their face in the water and losing sight of where they're going."

"Well, Gladys is nervous about getting her hair wet, so I don't know how you're going to talk her into it," I tell him, completely exasperated.

Cole bites back a smile. "I mentioned it in passing at bingo yesterday, and she didn't seem opposed to it."

"Oh, there's bingo available at this resort we're working at?"

"Yep," he says confidently. "It's a retirement dream, really. Warm weather. Dancing lessons. Soap operas are on constantly. Dinner's at four every night."

"It sounds like a regular person's dream, too. Which is why I didn't mind giving up my life here in the States to go for it."

"Same." Cole lets out an exaggerated sigh. "I got horribly sunburned the first week, though."

I cover my mouth, unable to stifle a yawn. "Well, that's why night swimming is preferred," I say simply. "No need to worry about SPF or tan lines."

"But risk of drowning if you're going to fall asleep in the pool," Cole teases.

"Sorry," I say, trying to shake off my tiredness. "I'm exhausted just thinking about Gladys."

"Trust me, I get it. Do you want to stop playing?"

"It depends," I toss back. "Do you feel better?"

He crosses his arms over his chest, but his expression is still relaxed. "Definitely."

"Good. Then yes, if that's okay, but I still want to float."

Cole glances upward. "It's a little cloudy tonight. You can't see all the stars."

I move my arms and legs in tandem to lift the front of my body to the water's surface. "Just because they're obscured at the moment doesn't mean they're not still there."

"Yeah," he says just loud enough for me to hear. "I guess you're right."

I keep my gaze fixed on the sky until I hear the slight splashing that indicates he's left me alone. Then I expel all the air from my lungs and sink below the surface, letting the water cover me completely.

NINE

It's hard to believe that the cartoon version of *Alice in Wonderland* was released half a century ago. But still, after all this time, it's holding my attention just as much now as it did when I was a kid.

Of course, all the animated Disney movies have to compete with the flashy CGI blockbusters that are the mainstay these days, but they will forever hold a certain place of nostalgia for me.

It's almost strange that I can watch something this old on a modern laptop, but I'm so "in" on it that I don't hear my mother calling for me until the impatience is clear in her tone.

"Allie!"

I jump up and open my bedroom door. "What?"

"Come here and help," she demands, then lets out an exhausted sigh.

"Help with what?" I call as I make my way down each step with a thud. "What's going on?"

Our kitchen is normally pristine and organized. But as I step in, I note several empty serving plates scattered about, an assortment of grocery bags at varying degrees of fullness, and multiple pans being monitored on the stove.

"The Kellers are coming over for dinner tonight," my mom says, stirring something that smells delicious and garlicky.

I blink. "What? They are?"

"I told you about this the other day, remember? Marlene and I want to start doing regular dinner parties."

"You didn't get it all out of your system last night?" I say with a snort.

"That was Sheila's birthday celebration," she says, batting her bangs off her forehead.

I ignore the reminder that my parents have more of a social life than I do.

"Can you help set the table?"

"Sure," I relent, opening the cupboard containing the dishes.

"You'll need seven," my mom adds.

"Seven?" I clarify as I hold four in my hands.

She bends down to check the chicken dish in the oven. "Yep. Us, Marlene, Kevin, Tess, and Cole. The whole crew is coming over."

I chew on my bottom lip as I take the plates over to the table. "What time?"

"About ten minutes," she says nonchalantly.

I move faster, grabbing the cutlery, napkins, and water glasses and organizing them accordingly. I hope expediting my pace will give me extra time to get ready so I don't just feel like a person who has been in their pajamas all day.

"Your dad should be back from the store to help shortly," she says; although, I think it's more for her reassurance than my benefit. "He forgot to get lemons."

"Lemons? For what?"

"Marlene and I are going to attempt to make sangria."

"Ah," I say, dropping the last fork in its place. "Okay, I'm going to go get ready."

Before she can give me another task, I rush up the stairs, internally panicking about what to wear.

I have a hard enough time choosing between three bathing suits under the cover of darkness. And now I need to find something that's somehow cute and flattering without looking like I'm trying too hard.

I step over the piles of clothing, books, and little knickknacks that litter my floor. I fling open my closet doors, stripping off my T-shirt and soft cotton shorts as I go. I should have done laundry today like I planned, but staying in bed seemed like a much better idea...

I tug on my favorite pair of ripped jeans, then pair it with an olive tank top that brings out the little flecks of green in my brown eyes.

My jewelry box is a chaotic mess, but I dig through for a pair of hoop earrings. The necklaces are all tangled, and I have to gently pull them apart until I free the most delicate rose gold one I own, then clasp it on.

I haven't worn either of these accessories since last summer, back when I wasn't fazed by the future. I was unconcerned with leaving, convinced that my relationships were infallible and happy to have a day at the mall with my mom's credit card.

Living in the present is kind of a bitch, though. My

"unrealistic expectations of a relationship" didn't become apparent until I was jolted to look back on it as decidedly in the past. Frankly, I was more devastated about the loss of friendships and the realization of my own naivety than I was about Lucas's actual cheating.

I wonder if Cole's friendships have survived the news of his father's treachery and jail time.

Given that I've never seen him texting on his phone, I doubt it.

The door to my bedroom swings open just as I've finished fluffing up my hair with dry shampoo, and I jump in surprise at the sight of Tess in the doorway.

"Cute," she assesses, scanning my room quickly. "For some reason, though, I thought you'd be a neat freak."

"Tess," I groan as she collapses on my bed.

I kick my dirty laundry on the floor toward my closet, the scoop down to try and put some of the clutter in its rightful place.

Thirty seconds of damage control doesn't make any difference, so I give up.

She rolls her eyes at my laptop screen. "You're watching this? Don't you get enough of Alice during the week?"

I close my computer and set it on my desk. "It's not the same thing."

"Uh-huh." Tess pulls on the cord for the window blinds, letting natural light pour in. "Obsessive much?"

It takes me a second to realize she's talking about my role and not the fact that I spent an hour today staring between the blinds watching Cole mow the lawn.

"Do you always make yourself at home wherever you are?" I ask her, putting my hands on my hips in frustration.

"Maybe I feel comfortable around you," she says.

I stop and blink.

She bursts out laughing. "Kidding, obviously."

"Hey," Cole says as he hits the top step in the hallway.

"Hey," I return casually.

He glances around the space, and I turn to mimic him, trying to see it through his eyes.

The walls are the same shade of white they were painted before we moved in, and they still are currently undecorated. There are a dozen holes where I once had pictures—memories of my old life—tacked up with push-pins, but they all went in the garbage last fall.

The only signs of personality in my space now are among my belongings scattered on the floor.

Cole shoves a hand in his pocket and leans on the door-frame, making no move to cross the threshold. "Nice room."

"Thanks," I say, though I doubt his sincerity.

"It's definitely not as nice as your place in Manhattan," Tess chimes in to tell him. "But a big step up from the basement, I can imagine."

Leave it to her to give uncalled-for honesty.

"Yeah," Cole agrees.

"What are the chances our moms will let us drink some of that sangria?" Tess asks, playing with the frayed edges of a decorative pillow.

"Slim to none," I admit. "Well, yours might, but definitely not mine."

"Seems like a challenge I'm up for," Tess says as she stands up. "Come on. Let's go before they beckon us as if we're peasants."

She loops her arm through mine.

It's a move that I don't expect or want, but I'm helpless to do anything other than follow her downstairs.

I glance over my shoulder at Cole as he trails behind us, and he offers me a raised eyebrow and a half-smirk.

"Lex," Marlene greets me, her lips already turning a darker shade from the wine. "Or should I say Alice?"

I smile as she brings me in for a big hug.

"Congratulations," she says proudly.

"Thank you," I reply.

"Isn't that wonderful, Kevin?" Marlene says to her husband. "We live next door to a *star*."

Normally, I'd be embarrassed by this attention, or think someone was making fun of me, but Marlene is so sweet and genuine, I can only give a modest chuckle.

"Congrats, Alexandra," Mr. Keller offers flatly.

"We should celebrate," Tess declares with a surprising amount of enthusiasm.

I shake my head. "No, it's okay, we already went out to—"

She elbows me in the side and waves toward the pitcher. "Celebratory sangria for all of us!"

"Of course!" Marlene says excitedly. "Let's get you set."

My mom grimaces. "Uh, sure. You can try some."

Marlene doesn't miss her reaction. "Oh, sorry. Is that not okay?"

Mom's gaze meets mine, and whatever she sees in my expression makes her shrug. "You know what? Go for it. It's nothing you won't be doing at school soon, anyway."

Right.

At college.

Where it's expected I'll attend parties with large quantities of alcohol and stay out late dancing. Participate in the totally normal activities that every other eighteen-year-old is really looking forward to this summer before their freshman year...

Tess doesn't hesitate to step forward and pour a large glass for me.

I try to pawn it off on Cole once it's placed in my hands, but he waves me off.

"I'm good," he says.

I hold the chilled glass awkwardly as Tess takes her first sip.

"This is great, Mrs. Sutton," she gushes. "Where'd you get this recipe?"

I'm a little taken aback at the sight of Tess being nice and complimentary while leading the charge in conversation and personal skills.

Apparently, my confusion shows.

"She's playing pretend," Cole says, bending down to whisper in my ear.

"And that means she's had a personality transplant?" I return quietly.

"I think she wants to soothe whatever's going on with her by drinking lots of wine, and while I'm not in the mood to do the same, I've definitely been there."

"You used alcohol to drown out your problems?"

He shakes his head. "Remember my brief stint with cigarettes?"

"Of course," I say with a frown.

"A vice to try and numb a problem. It didn't help, but I didn't have a reason to kick the habit until Marlene forbade it." He glances at Tess as she takes another large sip. "And now, Tess has me *and* Marlene to look out for her and make sure she's okay."

"That's...actually really thoughtful."

He nods. "We Kellers have our moments."

"Well, cheers to that, I guess," I say before taking a small sip.

"How is it?" Cole asks.

"Sour. And kind of weirdly muted. It's like something that once had flavor is trying to compensate for its lack of it now by being overly sweet," I decide before bringing the glass to my lips for another drink. "It also tastes like it's going to give me a pounding headache."

Cole laughs. "Sounds about right."

"Dinner's ready," my mom announces when the oven timer beeps. "Please, take your seats, and I'll bring everything over."

Even though the table is round and there's no designated head seat, she took the time to make little place cards for everything.

My dad snorts at the display. "Assigned seats, huh?"

I frown at his teasing words.

While I think they're a little silly and extravagant, I can appreciate the time and effort she put into making them.

I shuffle around until I'm in the correct chair, happy to find that I'm flanked by Marlene and Tess, with Cole directly across from me.

"Smells great," Marlene gushes as my mom sets down a plate of chicken using hot pads.

"Thank you," my mom returns.

To her credit, it really does look good.

It's definitely on the healthy side, with grilled chicken, an oversized salad, a brown rice and vegetable dish, and a plate of brown seed bread.

But the smell of herbs and garlic makes my mouth water.

"You know what this could use?" Tess ponders, swirling the liquid in her glass.

"The opinion of someone who is of legal drinking age and not relying on her mother's graciousness?" Marlene teases.

Tess waves her off. "Strawberries."

My mother smiles. "That's actually not a bad idea."

"I was only instructed to get lemons," my dad jokes.

"Or maybe blueberries," Tess continues as she drains half her glass in one sip. "Have you ever had sangria with white wine?"

"How do you know so much about this?" I ask her.

She shrugs. "Existing."

I roll my eyes.

"There," my mom says with a note of finality as she takes her seat. "Allie, can you start passing the salad around?"

"Sure."

I snag a portion for myself before handing the bowl to Marlene.

It takes her all of three seconds to give up on trying to wrangle the salad tongs, then she uses one of the utensils like a rake to push a heap of lettuce onto her plate.

"How is the play going so far, Lex?" Marlene asks, passing the bowl over to my dad.

"Good," I answer. "I have my first costume fitting on Tuesday."

"That's exciting."

I nod and smile at Marlene. "I saw the costume department steaming a few pieces, including that orange slip dress you donated. But I'm hoping I get to wear your prom dress."

"Is it in the script that Alice is the 1996 prom queen?" Tess asks snidely.

"You've probably read the script as many times as I have," I remind her, refusing to be baited by her tone.

My dad clears his throat. "So, Cole."

For some reason, those two words make me instantly nervous.

I glance at Cole for the first time since sitting down, something I've been actively trying not to do.

It's been a little difficult given that he's not only directly in my line of sight, but he's actually sitting in *my* seat at the table. It's the place where I've sat to do homework, celebrate every single birthday, and have important conversations with my parents—and he's just casually occupying it.

"Do you have plans for the fall?"

The collective shift in attention his direction gives me the opportunity to gawk at him.

Cole, to his credit, doesn't falter under the weight of so many eyes. If anything, he straightens up, taking on the persona of someone who is accustomed to chatting with people twice his age.

"I did have plans to go to school," he admits, setting down his silverware to address my dad properly. "But with everything going on with my father, I'm going to take some time and figure it out before I reapply for the spring semester."

"That's logical," my dad agrees.

"I thought so."

"Are you thinking of staying here, or will you be heading back to New York?"

"Dad, don't interrogate him," I jump in.

"I'm just trying to get to know him," he says innocently.

"It's okay," Cole says to me before smiling tightly. "I had planned on going to school in Connecticut, but now I'm not sure."

"Fair enough," my dad relents. "Have you been to many Yankee games, living in the city?"

Cole nods. "Yes. We used to have box seats."

Dad's eyes widen. "Big baseball fan, then?"

"I played at my school freshman and sophomore year," Cole says nonchalantly.

"He didn't just play," Mr. Keller cuts in. "He was recruited by a few colleges before he quit."

My dad, a lifelong Pirates fan, grins at this connection. "Oh, really? What position?"

"Shortstop," Cole answers.

That's new information.

But I guess it's not all that shocking.

I can see how he'd fill out a uniform with his swagger and build. Baseball getups are a little strange to me, with their long pants and tucked-in shirts, but on him, I think it might be kind of sexy.

I suppose it's odd to me, given that I feel this *connection,* that I don't know all these little details about him.

I can read his body language based on the way his

mouth ticks and his eyebrows twitch. I know that he prefers grape jelly over strawberry jelly. I sense that he's hiding layers of hurt and uncertainty from the world.

But I don't know anything, really, about his old life other than very surface details. The same goes for him with me, I suppose.

Cole and my dad start discussing this year's lineup, and I'm slightly floored that my dad has paid this much attention to a rival team.

The topic is boring enough that I take another drink of my sangria, just for something to do, and I immediately regret it. Tess swipes it from me as they chatter on, an act that is also caught by Marlene, but she doesn't say anything.

My mom must notice that Cole hasn't touched his meal out of politeness for the conversation because she cuts in to give him a break. "Are you excited for culinary school, Tess?"

"Absolutely," she says enthusiastically.

I glare at the girl next to me. "'Existing' is why you are good with recipes? Not because you're going to be a *chef*?"

She bats her eyes at me innocently. "All of the above."

"We should have teamed up for dinner tonight," my mom says with a smile.

"Definitely next time," Marlene says.

Tess, happily sipping on her drink, agrees, "That would be so unbelievably wonderful."

I can't help but laugh at her odd enthusiasm, and Cole, too, lets out a quiet chuckle as he meets my eyes. We're both in on the joke, but no one else is, taking her eagerness at face value.

"We're happy to have you all here for now," Marlene says. "We should do this a few more times before the summer ends."

"Cheers to that!" Tess says, clinking her glass—well, *my* glass—to her mother's.

"There doesn't seem to be any rush," Mr. Keller says gruffly. "By the looks of it, Cole will be here long-term. It's not like my brother is up to the task of child-rearing, considering he's left his boy homeless and disgraced."

Cole's knuckles go white as he tightens his grip on his fork, and I catch the subtle clenching of his jaw.

Whether she sees this or not, Marlene tosses back, "So? Lord knows you've never been fully on your feet. Are any of us, really?"

Cole smiles gratefully. "Thank you, Aunt Marlene."

She offers him an exaggerated wink.

"So, for our next dinner party, we should definitely do margaritas," Tess says to my mom.

They immediately begin brainstorming menu ideas, carrying the conversation along nicely.

By anyone else's estimation, the rest of dinner is pleasant and uneventful, but to me, it's a roaring success.

Mostly because Cole and I spend the majority of the meal exchanging looks, our own silent commentary on the dialogue around us.

And I decide I'd much rather have this type of conversation with him than talk to anyone else.

TEN

"Don't you dare speak," Tess growls, voice groggy and sunglasses fixed firmly in place.

I wondered how she'd fare after the overpoured glasses of sangria, and this morning, I'm getting my answer.

She crawls into the backseat of my Jeep, buckles in, and sprawls out as best she can. "Why does gravity have to exist today?"

"Gravity?" I repeat. "That's who you're blaming?"

Cole shakes his head as he slides into the passenger seat and closes the door.

"Did you have to slam it?" Tess snaps.

He glances over his shoulder. "I didn't—"

"No music, either."

"Fine," he breathes.

"Hi," I say quietly to Cole.

The corner of his mouth ticks up. "Hi."

Tess puts her hands over her ears. "No talking."

"You're going to have a hell of a time at rehearsal today if you can't even tolerate our two words," I tell her.

"Waiting for the pills to kick in," she grumbles.

I crack the window, wanting at least some noise to accompany us on the drive over to the theater.

She, thankfully, doesn't complain while Cole and I continue our game of silent conversation, catching each other's eye at every stoplight and exchanging small smiles.

When we arrive, we immediately split up.

Cole heads over to chat with Craig, who greets him warmly. Tess moves slowly toward the entrance, likely heading backstage to find a dark corner to sit in. I head straight to the stage, excited to begin rehearsing with movement.

We start off on a good note with the tea party, which has been morphed into a basement house party to be more relatable. It's my favorite scene of them all because it includes Andrew, Beau, Mike—who plays Dormouse—and a middle-schooler named Aggie who plays the Duchess.

I thought casting a thirteen-year-old was a strange choice, considering the character in the movie was played by a forty-something-year-old actor. But watching Aggie's talent and stage presence as she speaks in a high English accent only brings more charm to the entire production.

By contrast, I dread the scenes with Esme.

She's only in the play toward the end and delivers the "Off with her head!" with a frightening amount of enthusi-asm. It's the big bang in the production that sets off the chaos of arguing before I mock-faint.

In the book, that moment is the catalyst for Alice to wake up in her bedroom and realize Wonderland was all a dream. But for this version, after I pretend to collapse and am whisked off, I make a grand escape with the help of the White Rabbit.

The play ends with Alice standing at a crossroads, looking at the options ahead for her next grand adventure.

As she takes a decisive step, the lights dim, and the curtain drops.

For our rehearsing purposes, though, instead of walking through our bows, we simply all move toward the end of the stage where Joe is waiting to give us notes. I need to work on my projection in the party scene, and a few other actors have feedback on what they can improve on as well.

All in all, the show is coming together nicely, which is insane to think about, considering the short amount of time we've had to put it together.

I guess that's what's special about this program—the packed schedule means everything moves at a faster pace.

Before I know it, we'll be performing, and then it will all be over.

Tess is already waiting for me by my car when we wrap for the day. Her sunglasses are still firmly fixed in place, reflecting my figure as I approach and unlock the Jeep.

Cole has apparently taken ownership of the front seat—with a surprising lack of resistance from his cousin—and he's covered in sawdust and speckles of paint.

"That kind of looks like a constellation," I gesture to a row of three dots across his chest.

He glances down, and a genuine smile spreads across his face, causing my heart to stutter.

"Greasy food," Tess demands from the backseat.

"Was that a request, a suggestion, or a plea?" I ask, my eyes meeting hers in the rearview mirror.

"Don't mess with me, Sutton. I need carbs and butter and things that are going to fix this hangover and give me heartburn."

"Well, I need gas anyway," I tell her.

"Sheetz?" she says, brightening up a fraction. "Oh, please, with all the goodness in your heart, indulge me and chauffeur us to Sheetz."

"What the hell is Sheetz?" Cole asks incredulously.

I gape at him as I accelerate out of the theater parking lot. "The best gas station known to humanity. I can't believe you've never been."

"You're this excited about a gas station?" he clarifies, glancing over his shoulder at his cousin.

"You'll understand when we get there," she returns confidently.

"I actually agree with her," I admit. "It's a *thing* here. Seriously."

He shakes his head but doesn't offer another word as we continue on our way.

When we park, his pursed lips and furrowed brow tell me he's still skeptical. But as we step inside the bright, clean, spacious interior, his expression relaxes until he appears somewhat amused.

"Sheetz," he says quietly, starting down one of the aisles.

It's been a while since I've been in one of these. The closest gas station to my house is a rundown little shack of a thing with food that's well past its expiration, but this place is packed and just as cool as I remember.

I take in every type of chip and candy available on the shelves, then lead Cole toward the walk-up counter.

"You can get coffee, fried food, whatever you want," I tell him as I flip through the options displayed on a touchpad.

"What is a mac and cheese bite?" he asks, gazing at the screen over my shoulder.

"Only the best thing ever invented on Earth," Tess inserts, then she shoos my hand away and orders three servings. "This is my treat."

"Really?" I ask. "That's surprisingly nice of you."

She makes a big show of pulling a twenty-dollar bill out of her pocket. "Mom gave me this for gas money."

I snort. "And you planned on giving it to me when, exactly?"

"Now," Tess says, grabbing my hand. "Tell me what you want before I pick for you."

"Mozzarella sticks," I say quickly.

"Classic choice." She nods in approval. "Dipping sauce?"

I shake my head. "None."

"Now that's some serial-killer nonsense," she argues. "How are you going to have all that breaded cheesy goodness with nothing to cut it with?"

"I like them plain," I shrug.

"Well, I'm getting you boom-boom sauce if you change your mind," she says, making the selection.

"Do I even want to ask?" Cole drawls.

"It's like a peppery garlic mayo, I think," I explain. "I'm not a big fan of spicy food."

"And to think I was starting to come around to you,

Sutton," Tess tsks, shaking her head as she adds more food to our order. "Drinks?"

I shake my head. "I'm going to grab something from the cooler."

"Fine." She crosses her arms. "Cole, will you grab us a table?"

"Sure," he agrees, then heads off toward the seating area.

I grab bottled water for all of us. I approach the register, and I'm also unable to resist snagging a few chocolate bars and a pack of strawberry watermelon HubbaBubba.

"Here." I sit down across from Cole and offer the gum.

He takes the pack from my hand and traces the letters with his thumbs. "Thanks."

"Unfortunately, they didn't have cotton candy."

"This will do just fine," he says. "Although, I'm partial to the plain bubblegum flavor myself."

I smile, filing that information away for later. "Looking at that makes me nostalgic for all the candy I used to eat as a kid," I say wistfully. "When I managed to sneak it past my parents, at least."

"They're not big sweets people?"

"My mom's always been a bit of a health nut. Probably because she's a nurse and knows exactly how much diet impacts the body."

"Do you think she'd approve of using gas station food to cure a hangover?" Cole asks with a teasing grin.

I laugh and crane my neck to see how Tess is faring, but my stomach drops as I see who is standing beside her. "Oh no."

"What?" Cole asks, leaning out of the booth to follow my gaze.

"That's Gabriela with Tess," I inform him.

And by the looks of it, their conversation is not going well.

Tess has her hands on her hips, and the look of annoyance she usually saves for me is directed at her ex-girlfriend.

Gabriela, however, looks devastated.

She wrings her hands while she alternates between talking to Tess and biting her lip, clearly not getting what she wants from the conversation.

I promised myself I wouldn't pry, but it's hard not to want to.

"That doesn't look good," Cole mutters.

We slide back into the booth to give them privacy, even though they're facing off in the middle of the store.

"It doesn't," I agree. "I guess that's one benefit of not living close to my ex-boyfriend. Absolutely no chance of running into him."

"Oh?" Cole says the word innocently.

But I can tell by the way his eyes flash that he's curious for more details.

I decide to indulge him in hopes he'll feel comfortable enough to eventually do the same with me—just like how we volleyed questions back and forth.

"Yeah," I breathe. "We broke up after I moved here. He started, uh, dating my best friend. Well, former best friend. I haven't talked to either of them since Thanksgiving."

"That's why you're an expert in starting over," Cole says.

"Kind of," I admit. "I didn't mind the idea of moving originally because I thought, 'What's one more year when we're all moving away after graduation?' I didn't realize the consequences of my absence would be so great."

He fidgets with the pack of gum in his fingertips. "I tossed my phone after everything happened with my dad. Reading texts from people I thought were my friends, and getting messages on social. It was too much. I only kept the number of my best friend. Daniel. That's who I stayed with when I went back there for the trial."

"What's he like?" I ask, feigning casualness.

Cole smiles at whatever memory surfaces in his mind. "He's kind of mean, actually."

I bark out a laugh. "That's not how I tend to describe friends."

"He's got sharp edges, but he's the best," he continues. "The kind of guy who isn't afraid to tell you when you're being an idiot and would slap a person just for looking at him the wrong way."

"He's the male version of Tess, then?" I pose, running my fingers along the edge of the table. "On a normal day, at least."

Tess drops the tray on the table with a thud. "Who's the what?"

"Nothing," Cole says, apparently not wanting to rehash the details with her.

Or maybe she knows it all, anyway? I don't know.

She elbows me needlessly as I scoot. "Move over."

"Cole was telling me about his friends in New York," I explain.

She pops the lid on her chicken fingers. "How thrilling," she says emotionlessly.

I exchange a look with Cole before I clear my throat. "Are you okay?" I ask her.

She chews, and with each passing second, her hard facade slips. "No," she says once she swallows.

I reach over to pat her hand, but she flinches, so I pull back.

"Do you want to talk about it?" Cole asks.

"No." She sighs and pinches her eyes shut for a second. "Yes. Maybe. I guess."

Cole flicks open the collection of little bags on the table, evaluating all the food she ordered. "Well, we're going to be here eating for days, apparently, so whenever you're ready."

She cracks open one of the bottles of water and takes a pull. "My breakup with Gabriela was a mess. Originally, she was supposed to head up to school early, right after graduation, and that's why she broke up with me. She said she didn't want to 'put off the inevitable.' And then, when her plans changed, she told me she changed her mind. So I took her back, like an idiot, only to find out that she'd hooked up with Amanda Cline."

"Who's that?" Cole asks before he starts in on the french fries.

"My ex-girlfriend."

He winces. "Ouch."

"Yeah," Tess agrees. "And now she's having all these second thoughts about going to California for school, and she says I'm mostly why she doesn't want to leave...but I don't know if I want to be. Part of me is struggling to understand how she could do that, even if we were perma-nently broken up."

"It does seem like a lot of drama for what's supposed to be the best and easiest phase of our lives," I consider.

"If this is the best, then I'm screwed," Tess huffs, sniffling slightly.

"You'll figure it all out," I say reassuringly.

She rolls her eyes. "Of course *you* would say that."

I blink. "What do you mean?"

"You have this perfect life, Sutton," she says harshly. "Your parents are, like, obsessed with your happiness and well-being, and your dad moved jobs so you could go to freaking college for free. You act like you have all these problems, and you don't."

"Tess," Cole warns. "You're being an asshole."

She ignores him. "I get that it sucks that you had this, like, ridiculously embarrassing thing happen to you. But stop acting like you're wounded when you're actually the picture-perfect, doe-eyed girl next door who gets to run around in the spotlight like nothing ever happened."

I suck in my bottom lip, surprised at how much her words hurt. "So that's why you don't like me," I say. "You're..."

"Jealous," she supplies.

That's the last word I would have picked.

But judging by how pinched her expression is, I think she's being completely honest.

"Tess," Cole hisses between his teeth.

Tess lets out a breath and a low chuckle. "I would apol-ogize, but I actually think that was more painful for me to admit than for you to hear."

Laughter rumbles in my chest, but I don't let it out.

"I forgot napkins," she says, jumping up after making sure Gabriela is nowhere in sight.

The awkwardness she has created, the vulnerability that she's shown, has apparently become too much for her to tolerate.

Cole nudges my knee with his. "You okay?"

"Yeah," I say, releasing a breath.

"Good," he says, then double-checks that Tess is preoccupied. "I've been thinking about something."

I swallow a bite of my delicious and very plain mozzarella stick. "What's that?"

"That I want to see you. Like, more than just in the car and in the pool and watching you rehearse—"

"You watch me rehearse?" The question spills out of my mouth in surprise.

His cheeks redden slightly, like he didn't actually mean that to be the part I harped on. "Yes, of course, you know, when I'm bringing props in and stuff," he says quickly. "But I was wondering if you'd want to hang out or something tonight?"

I swear my soul smiles at his invitation. "Tonight?"

"If you're not busy," Cole says casually.

I've spent far too much time studying him this summer than I probably should have, but it pays off tremendously for my benefit.

Because from an outsider's perspective, he's all sly and nonchalant, but I catch the way his eyes drop slightly as he waits for my response.

He's *nervous*.

Which means he has something to lose.

He cares about me and, hell, is interested in me enough to want to spend his free time with me and hope that I'll agree to it.

"Leave the back door unlocked?" I suggest.

He brightens immediately. "I can do that."

"What's going on?" Tess asks as she sits down. "You're not harping on about Gabriela and me, are you?"

I don't know if it makes me a terrible person that I've pretty much forgotten all Tess's problems in favor of how insanely giddy I am.

Cole simply ignores her question and plucks a mac and cheese bite out of the bag. "Why are they triangles?"

Tess hears his question and is visibly grateful for the topic change as she resumes her seat, but she doesn't lose her attitude. "Who cares? They're delicious. Just enjoy it and don't overthink it."

For once, I actually agree with her.

ELEVEN

I've gotten too confident.

After so many weeks of sneaking into the pool every Saturday, the act of intruding on the Kellers' property doesn't faze me at this point.

I move on autopilot. My body knows the motions without my brain even actively thinking about it—so much so that, when I cross through the fence, I automatically move toward the stairs of the pool's shallow end.

I stop myself before I step in, remembering that I'm not in a bikini but donned in my favorite summer dress. It's yellow and off-the-shoulder, and it hits above my knees. It's bold enough that I don't feel like I have to play up my hair or jewelry but also casual and understated so I don't feel like I've dressed up just to sneak down into someone's basement.

I move toward the sliding back door, swiping my clammy palms on my dress before I pull on the handle. The panel squeaks slightly as it moves along the track. I step inside and close it behind me, lingering briefly to ensure the sound didn't carry down the hallway.

When the house remains silent, I breathe a sigh of relief and move deeper inside.

Cole left the basement door cracked, so I gingerly slip through it and close it behind me, cringing as I make my way down the creaky wooden stairs.

From how Marlene talks about this part of the house, I expect it to look like our basement—bare except for the washer, dryer, moving boxes, and cobwebs.

But as I take in the space, I'm pleasantly surprised at how nice it is down here, even though it has that chilly, underground feel.

Cole has carved out a niche for himself with a large area rug, framed by his twin bed and a small couch. His clothes are hung neatly along the wall on a rolling clothing rack. There's also a modern, free-standing lamp, along with a massive television, which is currently playing at low volume.

"Hey," Cole says, standing up to greet me.

"Hey," I return and nod to the screen. "Is this one of those cooking competition shows?"

He glances at the scene of someone frantically chopping parsley. "Yeah. Tess has got me hooked on them."

"I'm trying to imagine you and Tess casually watching something together, and I can't," I admit with a grin.

"You don't think we're one big, happy family?" Cole asks playfully. "I'm hurt."

I laugh, but it's a slightly nervous one because I don't know exactly how to do *this*.

Everything was easy with Lucas because we'd known

each other for so long. Our relationship was almost seamless, moving from friendship to more over time. We experienced all our firsts together, and it felt natural and wonderful—until it crashed and burned.

With Cole, it's not quite awkward, but I feel a little uncertain.

As much as I'm enjoying this back and forth of gazing and brushing against each other, I want more.

And I don't know how to achieve it.

I shake off all thoughts of my ex-boyfriend and lean into what feels right, taking a seat on the couch. I act like it's perfectly normal for Cole and me to be alone together at this time of night without the water as a barrier.

I watch the TV screen as the camera cuts away from the action to an interview with the contestant we'd just been watching, talking about what he'll do with the money if he wins.

"The old guy is totally going to win this round," I murmur.

"No way," Cole argues, turning up the volume slightly. "It's definitely going to be the woman in the middle. You missed her appetizer. It was so much better than all the others."

"The entrée carries more weight."

"I don't know about that. I mean, dessert seems to be what really clinches it. As long as no one tries to make ice cream."

As we get pulled into the antics and chef commentary, we get a little more comfortable with each other.

It's a logical progression for our thighs to touch, for me

to relax into the cushions and take in the scent of his shampoo at this proximity.

The final seconds count down as the chefs rush to finish their plating.

I squirm in anticipation watching them, only for that to be the exact moment Cole reaches over and tangles our fingers together.

The deliberate contact sends an electric charge throughout my body, but I maintain my outward coolness. It becomes increasingly difficult as his thumb rubs slowly and gently against mine, making me want to pass out and explode at the same time.

I somehow survive the torment, and when the winner is announced onscreen and my pick is selected, I laugh proudly.

"I knew it!" I exclaim.

Cole squeezes my hand. "You were right."

"Maybe someday Tess will be on the show," I muse, scooting back so I can tuck my leg under my thigh as I turn toward him.

"She's mentioned the possibility before." He pauses to smirk. "Well, she mostly talked trash about how much better she could do than everyone else."

I laugh. "That sounds like her."

"More power to her," he shrugs. "I could never do something like that."

"Be on television, or make a three-course meal?" I ask playfully.

"Both, absolutely. But you've already done one of those, so maybe you'll be competing against Tess."

"Oh, no," I deflect. "Cooking is too much guesswork. I

feel like I'd need directions. Maybe I'll be on that British baking show everyone obsesses over."

"And what is your baked good of choice?" he asks. "What does Gladys come by for every morning after her swim lesson?"

I shake my head. "I'm not a baker in Tahiti."

"Oh?"

"I've decided it's too warm there," I tell him. "I need someplace I can change the menu for the seasons."

"Pumpkin-flavored offerings in the fall?" Cole guesses.

"And peppermint and the other holiday flavors in the winter." I chew my lip as I consider possible locations. "I think I have a little bakery in New York. The Upper West Side."

"That makes sense," he agrees. "So you're catering to the family-friendly crowd? By the museums or the water? How far uptown?"

I don't know enough about the neighborhoods to answer that question, but I consider it. "I think profit-wise, I should focus on how to get people in who don't want to sit there for hours, taking advantage of free internet during the day. What if I want to be a late-night dessert purveyor to the drunk college crowd?"

"Looking for people who are hungry and forgiving?"

I grin. "Exactly."

"What about the Village? Or maybe somewhere in Brooklyn."

"I'm open to either," I say to him. "My award-winning peanut butter chocolate chip brownies will sell just fine in either borough."

Cole gives me a look of total exasperation. "Well, what about me?"

My heart flips. "What about you? What are you doing in this scenario?"

"Your taste-tester, obviously," he says easily.

"A risk."

"But worth it."

He brings our joined hands up to his mouth and presses a brief kiss on the back of my knuckles.

I startle slightly, as that little gesture changes the dynamic in an instant.

It's a reminder that we're able to touch each other, and that he *wants* to do things like this with me.

"You know, when I came here, I wasn't prepared for this," Cole admits quietly.

I brace myself. "What do you mean?"

He rubs his thumb over my knuckles as he meets my eyes. "I was pretty depressed and lost in my own head. I mean, the future I had worked so hard for and planned was stripped away from me. Within the span of a day, I went from a normal, prospective Yale student to getting hundreds of messages telling me I was a horrible person… all through no active fault of my own. I feel like it's impossible to realize when something is going to change you completely, but I knew it as soon as the handcuffs closed around my dad's wrists."

"I'm sorry," I tell him sincerely.

He swallows before he continues. "The FBI kicked me out of our home, and I honestly didn't know what to do with myself. I hid out at Daniel's house for a few days. But his family lost a lot of money when my dad went down.

Apparently, my dad had convinced them to do some bad investing. So Daniel's dad called CPS to get me 'out of his house.' Kind of as revenge, I guess, which is how I ended up here. Next of kin and all that."

"Wow," I breathe.

"Didn't see any of it coming," Cole says. "But now that I'm here, it's not horrible."

"Thank goodness for that," I say lightly.

Cole smiles. "I mean it, Alexandra. I was practically a zombie, miserable and alone, and then I met you, and everything changed."

I do the only logical thing a person can do after a declaration like that.

I lean forward, heart fluttering in my chest, and kiss him.

His reaction is immediate, meeting my gesture with lips that are so warm and soft.

He tastes faintly like bubblegum—a fact that makes me smile in the brief moment we part to adjust and move closer together.

I reach for him again, locking my hands behind his neck as he grips my hips and pulls me onto his lap.

My entire body melts as his fingertips move in circles on the bare skin of my shoulders.

He kisses me like it's the only thing keeping him going, and I can't help but pull back briefly.

I want to see what he looks like in this state, and I'm not disappointed. I'm awarded his most genuine grin yet, paired by his flushed cheeks and serious gaze.

He brings his pointer finger up, tracing a line from my cheek down to my jaw. "You have freckles," he whispers.

"They come out in the sun," I explain hoarsely.

He trails kisses all along them before capturing my mouth again.

This is what we should have been doing all along, not wasting time asking questions in a pool but exploring each other.

Screw the night sky. We don't need it because the movement between us alone causes me to see stars.

The basement door creaks open, jolting us out of our embrace.

"Cole?" Marlene says as she steps down the stairs.

I roll off his lap, and with nowhere for me to run or hide, he simply covers me with a blanket.

"Aunt Marlene, you're still up?" Cole asks, trying to come off nonchalant.

His lips are swollen and he is overall completely mussed, looking the furthest thing from innocent.

"Wanted to check and make sure you're okay," she says, tone sickly sweet. "And that you're going to bed soon. Early day tomorrow and all that."

"Yeah," he says while attempting to smooth his hair. "Planning on it."

"I mean *alone*," Marlene adds. "Without the Lex-shaped lump beside you."

I groan and pull the blanket down over my eyes. "Hi, Marlene."

She chuckles. "You know, I expected more from you, Lex. For an actor, you're sure not great at playing dead."

I laugh at that. "You're right."

"I'll keep this little rendezvous between us, but head out soon, okay?" Marlene says.

"Okay," I agree with a nod.

Marlene offers a final smile before heading back up. "Goodnight, you two."

Once the door closes again, I pull the blanket over my head, slightly mortified at getting caught.

Cole pulls at the fabric until he's cocooned under it with me.

"Worth it," he murmurs.

I hang up my dress after rehearsal on Friday, and in my mind, it officially marks the close of another *long* week.

But I am a little sad to say goodbye to Alice for the weekend, even though it means I get to use all my free time to catch up on sleep and sneak over to the basement again.

I smile at the baby blue ballgown as I pull down the protective plastic cover, ensuring no dust will even think about marring the beautiful fabric.

It's the same dress that Marlene wore to prom, but it's been altered to fit me. The hem is purposely chopped unevenly at my knees, leaning into the edgier vibe of the production. The costume designer kept the sleeves, which are puffed out and a little silly, but assured me they'll be balanced out by the combat boots and various other accessories added throughout the play.

The final result does kind of look like a 1990s getup, but from what I've read in fashion magazines, it works as well now as it did back then.

"You coming out?" Andrew asks as he hangs his own costume up beside mine.

I take the top hat off his head and put it on the shelf. "Coming to what?"

"I swear, Alexandra, you *repel* socialization," he says with a huff. "Mouse is having a party. It's all everyone's been talking about all day."

"I can't believe everyone refers to 'Mike' as 'Mouse.' And that he goes along with it."

"He likes having a nickname, especially one that's inspired by the character he's so fantastic at playing."

"That's good," I say, sliding my purse over my shoulder.

"But that's not the point here," Andrew insists. "Party. Mouse's house. Please come."

I frown because I don't know if I have plans with Cole.

We haven't clarified anything after the whole "Marlene walked in on us" thing.

Our time in the basement was incredible, delightful, and so many other adjectives, but I've gone home and crashed every single night this week, which hasn't lent well to a repeat performance.

So aside from the car rides, lunches, and quick glances shared when he happens to bring set pieces onstage, we haven't seen much of each other this week.

"I don't know what my plans are yet," I tell Andrew.

"Apparently, the entire crew is coming," he presses in an attempt to sway me. "So if you're trying to decide based on that hot blond guy with a saw who has been staring at you all week, chances are he's in."

"Well, considering I have to drive him and Tess everywhere, it might be up to me."

"Even better!" Andrew gushes. "You can't miss this. It's tradition."

"To have a party at Mouse's house?" I ask.

"No. For whatever reason, it's become a thing that instead of doing a big cast party at the end of the show, we do a 'Set and Dress Success' party. It's because we—"

"Successfully completed the set and a week of dress rehearsals?" I interrupt.

"See? You get it. It's like a bonding experience and a blow-off-steam session all at once. Because next week is when the process starts getting really tedious."

"It's not tedious yet?" I mutter. "We had to practice the same scene *seven* times today."

"Imagine when we need to start making tweaks to costumes and change all the blocking we just memorized because of how the set looks."

"Yes." Tess saunters in and dumps her headset and battery pack on the counter. "Party at the Mouse House tomorrow."

I quirk a brow at her. "Oh yeah?"

"Hey, are you ready to—" Cole stops at the threshold, eyeing the three of us.

"Sutton," Tess looks at me seriously. "We are going to the party, and we are going to blow off steam, and we are going to enjoy it."

"I don't know," I start.

"And we are going to *not* drink sangria," Tess adds.

She and Andrew both stare at me expectantly. "Fine," I relent. "At least I won't have to deal with another Tess hangover."

"But you will have to deal with my drinking games," Andrew counters. "Which are awesome, by the way."

"See?" Tess says. "No problems at all. Just your average teenage debauchery."

I glance at Cole, trying to gauge his thoughts on these plans.

He shrugs. "What could go wrong?"

————

I could take Cole's flippant response as a sign that something bad is in my future.

But I don't.

Because I'm swept up in running through possible outfit ideas and wondering what kind of trouble all the theater kids and crew members are going to get into.

If anything, I allow myself to get excited by the prospect of attending a real party—something I haven't done since moving to this town. Mostly because I haven't been invited.

However, when I step into the kitchen, I discover my parents have other plans for me.

Usually, if they're both home at this time, they're sitting in the living room, watching mindless television or reading with soft music playing in the background.

Although now that I think about it, I can't remember the last time I saw them together aside from mealtimes. My mom's been picking up a ton of extra shifts, trying to look good for her new bosses at the hospital, and my dad's preoccupied with planning fall classes and stressing over getting tenure.

And so, as much as I want to breeze past them both, I

stop immediately, hovering in the middle of the room as I take in their change of routine.

One look at their stilted posture at the kitchen table tells me they want to talk.

And it's not going to be a good conversation.

"What's going on?" I ask as I drop my purse on the counter.

I don't know if it's my question or the jarring thud of my bag that jolts them from staring at the tabletop, but they both turn to face me simultaneously.

"Come sit down, Allie," my mom says, voice devoid of emotion.

"Is everything okay?" I glance between them.

My dad nods and smiles like some sort of pod person, and it doesn't encourage me.

I immediately go to the darkest place imaginable. "Is one of you…sick? Is someone hurt? What's happening?"

"No, no." My dad waves his hand. "We're perfectly healthy and okay, and everything is going to be fine."

"But we do have something we want to talk to you about," my mom adds.

"Okay," I say slowly as I finally sit down.

"Look," she begins, "there's no easy way to say this—"

"Say it," I interrupt. "Please just tell me what's going on."

They exchange a glance before my dad opens his mouth. "We're getting divorced."

I squeeze my eyes shut, as if that will help me process the information.

My parents have been my rocks my entire life. They've

been endlessly supportive of my pursuits, even when I've wanted to quit.

It's always been the three of us, our own little family unit, planning for the future and being together.

And now my world has shifted.

"Why?" I blurt out, taking in their concerned expressions. "When? I don't..." I trail off, at a loss for words.

My dad reaches for my hand, but before he makes contact, I put my palms on my thighs.

"I don't need to be comforted," I tell him, knowing that doing so will make me break down. "I just need to understand what's going on."

"Sometimes people grow apart, Allie," my mom reasons.

I shake my head. "But how? You've been together my whole life. What changed so suddenly?"

"Nothing changed," she explains. "It happened over time."

I sink my teeth into my bottom lip, trying to use pain to cancel out the sheer helplessness that's causing tears to form in my eyes.

"Alexandra," my dad says firmly. "We've been heading this way for a while. We thought the change of location could be good for all of us."

"But it didn't work out that way," my mom says. "And that's okay. Because your dad and I will always love each other, and you're our top priority."

My phone buzzes on the table, and even though I know it's rude to do so, I glance at it.

It's Tess informing me that some people are already at

Mouse's and that we should head out sooner rather than later.

I take a deep breath, grateful for the distraction from all this heaviness.

The party that I was lukewarm about to begin with now feels like a life raft.

It's selfish of me, I know, not to offer any words of support to my parents. Their lives are definitely going to change as much as mine in this situation.

Like, who is going to move out? Are we going to split Christmas celebrations moving forward? Who is going to show up to parents' day at school?

I shake off my questions because no matter the answers, they will cause me to have a complete emotional spiral, and the last thing I want to be at this party is the girl who is a drunk, emotional mess.

"I'm sorry," I say, rubbing my eyes with the heels of my hands. "I have plans tonight, and this is way, way too much for me to process right now."

"It's okay," my mom says reassuringly. "Nothing is changing right now, nor does it need to."

My dad nods in agreement. "We've been waiting for the right time to tell you."

I hold back my scoff.

I don't think there's ever a right time for this, but I don't vocalize that opinion.

One thousand thoughts are bouncing around in my head, and I want to process exactly none of them.

I shoot a response to Tess as I head upstairs to the safe haven of my bedroom. *I'll be ready in thirty minutes.*

Her reply is instantaneous. *Fashionably late, but not too much that we'll miss most of the party. I like it.*

The timeframe gives me enough time to take a quick shower, washing off the day and the conversation with my parents. I forgo makeup in favor of curling my hair in haphazard waves, conscious of the minutes ticking by.

I reach for a cute pair of denim shorts and a tank top that is a size too small, giving the impression that I'd actually willingly spend money on a crop top. After securing a pair of earrings and sliding on a few bracelets, I deem myself finished.

I think I've successfully created an illusion to hide how I'm feeling inside.

THIRTEEN

"And where exactly are you off to?"

"Marlene," I nearly shriek as I close the front door of my house and step on the front lawn.

She steps toward me, eyes appraising my outfit. "Where are you going in *that*?" she asks, smiling coyly.

I glance down at my outfit, noting that while I am showing more skin than usual, I don't feel self-conscious about it. I feel *good*, actually.

And I want a night to just play pretend that everything is fine and enjoy it.

"A party," I tell her simply.

"A party?" Marlene repeats.

I nod. "Yes."

"I see." She crosses her arms over her chest. "And would that happen to be the same party that Cole and Tess have been fussing over?"

"That's the one," I admit.

"Well, good," Marlene says. "Because I'd hate to think that Tess stole an entire bottle of vodka only for herself."

I snort, thinking I wouldn't put it past her.

"You kids should be out enjoying yourselves after all the work you've been putting in," Marlene continues. "Especially you, Lex. You deserve a night out."

I try to return her enthusiasm, but I fail. "Thanks," I say flatly.

She tilts her head, assessing me. "I'm guessing your parents told you the news."

My lungs burn as I try to keep my emotions buried. "Yes," I manage, unsurprised that Marlene knew about this before I did.

"Oh, Lex," she says, pulling me in for a hug.

I appreciate the gesture, but I don't give in to it completely, trying to keep my sadness in check.

"I guess this means all dinner parties are canceled," I offer.

She chuckles and pats my back.

Once she releases me, she puts one of her perfectly manicured nails under my chin and lifts my face so I can look her in the eye.

"Go out and enjoy the night," she tells me. "Don't let the adult stuff get you down."

"Thank you," I say gratefully as I start moving.

"And no driving if you plan on drinking," she calls after me.

I grimace at her volume as I jog toward my car where Tess and Cole are already waiting for me.

"Wow," Cole mouths upon my approach.

His wide eyes and genuine reaction spark an actual

smile on my lips, which is something I doubted I'd find this evening.

"Your parents let you wear that?" Tess asks doubtfully, eyeing my appearance.

I frown. "I don't know whether to be more offended that you're insinuating what I'm wearing is inappropriate or that I let other people hold any control over what I wear."

She rolls her eyes and opens the door to the Jeep, sliding in the back. "I'm not trying to be a bitch, you know."

"Maybe you should try harder," I snap.

Tess laughs. "Someone's in a mood."

I sigh and regret my words immediately. "Sorry."

"Whatever," she says, waving her hand. "Let's get the hell out of here."

"Do you know where you're going?" Cole asks.

"I've got the address," Tess inserts, plugging it into her map app. "It's in the swanky part of town."

Cole smirks. "Swanky?"

"What? It's a good word."

"Yeah, if you're forty-five," Cole retorts.

"Swanky, swanky, swanky," Tess rapid-fires just to annoy him. "What kind of music do you have queued up for us, Sutton?"

"Uh..."

Tess reaches for my phone, scrolling through my playlists before settling on the rock-heavy one. She then spends the fifteen-minute drive alternating between giving commentary on my music choices and directing me toward the right place.

But all three of us fall silent as we take the final turn into the neighborhood.

The houses have to be four times the size of mine. They're all pristinely decorated and have the thing called *curb appeal* I've learned about on home renovation shows.

Tess leans forward, pressing her body between the front seats to get a better view. "It's the one straight ahead, at the end of the street."

I follow her guidance and pull onto the property. The driveway is long enough that we're tenth in the line of parked cars, but there's still nearly double the space left behind us.

"Swanky," Cole murmurs.

"Told you," Tess says proudly as we step out.

I tangle my fingers in my tendrils as Tess charges forward.

"You okay?" Cole asks, sliding his hand on my lower back.

I warm at the welcome contact. "I am now."

The corner of his mouth ticks up as Tess knocks. "Good."

"Welcome," Mouse says, opening the double front doors.

Instead of a nervous, fumbling mess, he waves us into his home with a half-full cup of beer, taking confidence in his own space.

Tess lets out a low whistle at the impressive interior, offers him a salute, then takes off at a fast walk.

Before Cole and I can follow, Mouse steps in our path.

"Keys, please," he says, holding out his hand.

"Oh," I say, surprised.

"My parents only agreed to let me do this if no one was driving," Mouse tells me.

This is probably information Andrew or Tess or *anyone* should have shared with me, but with Marlene's encouragement in mind, I relent.

"Here." I hand them over, feeling an instant relief from the burden of having to be the responsible one all the time.

Normally, I would be in my head about staying out all night and drinking, but tonight, I'm ready to let it all go.

"Drinks are in the kitchen," Mouse says, dropping my key ring in a bowl in the entryway.

"Cool, thanks for having us over," Cole replies, then grabs my hand and pulls me along. "I can drive us home if you want."

"Do you even have your license?" I ask him.

He pretends to be offended by my question. "Of course. What do you think I am?"

"Some spoiled brat New Yorker," Tess answers for me.

The rest of the cast is around the massive island covered in the liquor bottles, cups, and various chasers.

"Are you sure you want to stay?" Cole asks as he eyes the spread. "I can seriously drive us home if you want."

"I appreciate the offer." I lean over and drop my voice. "But tonight, I want to play pretend."

"Oh?" His eyes flash. "What's the setup?"

"We're two normal teenagers who don't have to deal with the big question mark that is the future or all the shit our parents are putting on us or expectations or anything else."

He quirks an eyebrow but doesn't question me. "Okay."

"Here," Tess says, pushing a cup into my hands. "This doesn't even taste like alcohol."

I wrinkle my nose. "What is it?"

"A lot of alcohol."

I take a sip, relieved it tastes more like Sprite and juice than anything else. "Thanks."

She hands one to Cole, who glances at me for a final check.

I give him an encouraging nod, then the three of us cheers and drink.

"Hey, hey, hey," Andrew says, sauntering into the kitchen. "Wasn't sure if you were coming, Alice."

I smile. "Am I supposed to call you 'White Rabbit' all night?"

"Well, to your point, it's only fair if Mouse is always identified as his character."

"He's definitely been typecast," Esme sneers, finally making her appearance. "Such a little mousey thing."

She laughs like it's a joke, but aside from her little group of loyal followers, no one else does as she helps herself to a generous pour of alcohol.

"In fact, I think we've all been put in our place quite well," Esme assesses. "Andrew, you're a great choice for such a twitchy, hoppy thing. And poor little Aggie who is too young for a party is right for the crazy Duchess."

"And I suppose you think you make a perfect queen," I bite out.

"Better than an annoying, indecisive Alice," she says smugly.

"Hey, Esme," Tess calls for her attention.

Esme takes another sip. "What?"

"Shut the hell up."

I almost choke on my drink as Cole and Andrew both laugh.

Esme glares at the group of us. "Funny."

"Wow, this house is amazing, like some serious *Great Gatsby* shit," Beau says, appearing with Mouse trailing behind.

"Hey," Mouse says defensively before laughing.

"They mean you're classic," Tess insists, pouring more vodka into her mixed drink.

Mouse smiles. "I guess I can deal with that."

"Who wants to play a game?" Beau asks as they fill up their own cup.

"Maybe me," Tess says. "Do you have a deck of cards?"

"Oh, uh, I'm not sure." Mouse goes to one of the kitchen drawers and opens it.

Apparently, no matter how big and beautiful a house is, there's always a junk drawer.

Mouse shakes his head. "I don't think we have any."

"Quarters?" Tess suggests.

"What about flip cup?" Cole asks, eyeing the towering collection of red plastic cups.

"Perfect. Everyone, line up." Tess directs some of the others over to the opposite side of the island. "Esme, you're on that side."

Esme rolls her eyes but obliges.

Beau and Mouse measure out equal pours of drinks in the cups lined up on the counter, ensuring no one has an advantage over anyone else.

"Okay, when I say 'go,' you're going to chug your

drink," Tess instructs. "And when you finish, you're going to put your empty cup down and flick it like this—"

She demonstrates how the move is done, and of course, expertly flips it on the first try.

"Any questions? No? Good. Let's do this in three...two...one...GO!"

Cole, on my left, is the first to do so, downing his drink and successfully flipping his cup on the second try.

I have less success with mine, but I laugh as my team cheers me on while Tess screams pointers.

When I finally land it, I look up to see Esme's irritation grow as her friends from the makeup crew spend more time giggling than trying to win.

Our team continues the relay. Tess and Beau get through theirs quickly, but Andrew has even more trouble than I did.

He finally successfully rights his cup, and I jump up and down in excitement, then am rewarded with Cole wrapping his arms around my waist.

Just as Esme, who's only third in line on her side of the counter, finishes her drink and wipes her mouth, Mouse flips his cup on our side for the win.

He crushes the plastic in his hand as we all cheer and bring him into the middle of a huddle for a hug.

It's probably the most excitement Mouse has ever had in his life, and we all pump him up, happy that he was the one to make us victors.

The losing team mostly shrugs it off as we celebrate obnoxiously and head to the living room, where the other partygoers are swaying and singing along to the music that's playing.

"Congratulations, everyone," Esme drawls. "You've officially been good at one thing in your life."

"Don't be a sore loser," Tess says with an eyeroll.

Esme sniffs. "As if I would let some stupid, meaningless game have that big of an impact on me."

"We get it, Esme, you're channeling the whole bitchy mean girl thing. It's working for you." She pauses and smiles ruefully. "But if you're so much better than us, then why are you even here?"

"I was doing you a favor by showing up," Esme bites out.

"You'll do a better one by leaving," Tess says, squaring up with her.

Esme smirks and downs the rest of her drink without a flinch. "Come on, girls, let's get out of here."

"Thank god," Tess says to our core crew once she's gone. "Let's get back to the point of this, yeah? We are having *fun*. We are blowing off *steam*."

She winks at me as I polish off my drink.

"Right, Sutton?"

"Right," I agree. "So, what do we do next?"

Mouse smiles widely. "Anyone up for a swim?"

FOURTEEN

The clothes come off as we all grab our bottles and cups and head to the backyard.

And what ensues is a mess of drinking, discarded shirts, and laughter—it's the teenage party montage I never got to experience myself until now.

I don't overthink it as I strip down to my bra and underwear, grateful that I'm wearing articles I feel somewhat comfortable in. Though I do admire how fearlessly Tess rocks her lace bra and high-cut bikini underwear set.

"Here," she says, handing me a bottle. "Drink and pass."

I do, taking a swig directly from the container before I hand it over to Mouse, and the succession continues.

Once we've all gulped down enough alcohol to feel it charging through our veins, we dive into the water.

I immediately move to the shallow end, finding that I'm even worse at swimming in an inebriated state. It's unsurprising, of course, but still a little disappointing given how much fun everyone else is having splashing around.

Cole appears at my side, letting the waves from the others' activity bring us close enough to touch.

"Enjoying yourself?" he asks in a low tone.

I exhale, suddenly wishing that it was just the two of us in the Kellers' pool.

"This is *warm*," Tess calls up toward the sky as she backstrokes.

"Are you sure it's not just the alcohol clouding your mind?" Beau suggests with a laugh.

Mouse shakes his head as they all slowly swim toward shallower waters. "No, I cranked up the temperature in anticipation of this moment."

Tess snorts. "So you were hoping that we'd all sloppily fall half-naked into your pool?"

"I, uh—"

"I'm kidding," she interjects.

I can see Mouse's blush with help from the fancy bulb lights that are strung up around the yard.

"Who wants to play a game?" I ask, changing the subject.

"Twenty questions?" Cole poses with a wry smile.

Andrew bobs beside me. "Marco Polo or sharks and minnows?"

"Neither," Tess decides firmly. "Truth or dare."

Cole groans. "Seriously?"

"Oh, come on," she says. "Don't tell me you're still mad about the last time we played."

"Mad? Absolutely not. Forever embarrassed? Yes."

"What happened?" I ask curiously.

Cole shakes his head and slides a hand on my waist. "Nothing you need to know about."

I quirk a brow. "Now I'm even more intrigued."

"So are we playing or what?" Tess huffs.

"Absolutely," Beau agrees, glancing at the enthusiastic nods of Andrew and Mouse. "Who goes first?"

Tess grabs the vodka bottle from the edge of the pool and takes a swig. "Me. Oh, and as a rule, when it's your turn, you have to take a big drink."

"Sounds like a very safe activity for us to be playing in a pool," I tease.

"Shut it, Sutton," she says, but her tone is surprisingly light. "Okay, I choose Mouse. Truth or dare?"

"Dare," he says immediately.

"That was a decision made with confidence. I like it." She pauses and considers him. "I dare you to go into your house and bring out as many bags of chips as you can carry."

"Boring," Andrew calls.

"I'm getting hungry," Tess admits with a laugh. "But fine. I dare you to go inside and start dancing in the middle of the group."

"Easy," Mouse says, moving toward the stairs.

"And no adding clothes," she calls. "You have to dance in your skivvies."

If Mouse is embarrassed by strutting back inside dripping wet in his Batman boxers, he remarkably doesn't show it.

We all watch through the windows as the crowd inside whoops for Mouse as he jumps in the center of their circle, sending drops of water all around him.

I like to think that we've all grown as performers since the play began, but there's no doubt in my mind that Mouse has benefitted the most.

He gains more confidence with each rehearsal, hitting his mark and lines with purpose and pride every single time. The repeated praise from all of us, and Joe himself, has done wonders to help him act less nervous.

The person he was at the beginning of all this would never have had the guts to dance like a robot at a party, I'm sure of it.

When he comes back a few moments later, he takes a bow, and we all clap for him.

"Well done," Tess praises, handing him the bottle. "It's your turn to pick someone."

Mouse winces at the taste, then locks eyes with each person, like he's trying to make us all nervous about who his victim will be.

"Cole," he decides. "Truth or dare?"

"Truth," Cole says as the little waves move around us. "I'm not as good of a dancer as you are, nor do I want to be subjected to such cruelty."

"Fair enough." Mouse smiles as he swirls the bottle around in his hand, buying time to come up with a question. "What are you afraid of most in the world?"

It's far too serious a query for a drunken pool party, but I already know Cole isn't going to back down from answering honestly.

Tess and I are the only ones who know Cole's real reason for being here this summer, and I'm not sure if the others anticipate the heaviness of that truth—or have awareness of how it likely ties to his answer.

"Well, I assume we're taking 'Are we spinning around on a rock in space for any real reason?' type of thoughts off the table?" Cole verifies.

"Assumption agreed upon," Mouse nods.

Cole sinks below the surface, letting the water cover him all the way up to his collarbones. He's using the water as a shield, like he's guarding his heart from acknowledging the pain of losing his mother or the shame of what his father has put him through.

My own answer to this question would be something cheesy and embarrassing. Like voicing my concern for my previous loss of passion or hope in the future I've created for myself.

But Cole surprises me.

"Butterflies," he says quietly.

Tess cackles. "What? No way."

"That's...ridiculous," Mouse sputters. "We're, like, ten times their size!"

"You asked for the truth, and that's it," Cole says with a smile.

"What about them terrifies you?" I ask. "The fluttery beauty they bring to the world? Or how they can completely transform themselves to make their own way like no other creature on the planet can?"

He blinks. "Well, when you put it that way..."

"Boring," Tess singsongs. "But very poetic and whatever. Who's next?"

"Alexandra," Cole says, turning to me with a devilish smile.

It's such a small thing, but I love that I'm the one he picks.

"Dare," I tell him with a challenging look.

"I dare you to tell us all something about your life as a child star that you've never shared with anyone," he says.

"Ooh, yes!" Beau excitedly agrees. "Spill all the Hollywood secrets."

I'm surprised by how much I don't mind the idea of talking about that here, like it's something worth sharing among friends when it's not being whispered about behind my back.

But because my fame happened when I was young, I didn't exactly pick up on a lot of cool stuff, but there is one little piece of gossip I can share.

"Are you familiar with who all starred in *Wanda*?" I ask.

Beau guffaws. "It launched, like, eight A-lister careers. So yes."

"Right." I pause just to build the anticipation. "Well, one of them was my first kiss."

"What?" Tess nearly shrieks. "But so many of those people are, like, ten years older than us."

I shrug, not bothering to reveal that it was the costar of mine who is exactly the same age.

Just because I picked truth doesn't mean I have to solve the mystery for them.

"Whoever it was, they were probably better than my first kiss," Beau says wistfully. "Mine happened in the back of the bus on the way to band camp freshman year."

"Who was yours?" I ask Cole after most of the others share their stories.

"An ex-girlfriend," he says flatly. "It was very serious."

I try to pretend like that sentence doesn't make me want to double over. "Oh?" I breathe.

"Yep. Our wedding was at recess in fifth grade, and we had rings made out of grass and everything."

I let out a laugh. "A married man, then? I feel so deceived."

Mouse clears his throat. "I've never been kissed."

"It'll happen when it happens," Andrew tells him reassuringly.

He nods and smiles sadly. "I don't know. I'm eighteen and about to go off to college. It's a little embarrassing. Like, what if I do it wrong or something?"

Tess takes another swig of vodka, then doggy paddles over to him, wrapping her arms around his neck.

"Well?" Tess says. "I'm going to need some sort of confirmation you're on board with this."

He doesn't lose the disarming look of surprise on his features as he nods.

She yanks him down toward her, then kisses him gently.

He freezes until she deepens the kiss, then he comes back to his own body, closes his eyes, and tries to keep up with her rhythm.

"Is it weird that I'm happy with what's happening right now?" Cole asks quietly. "I mean, this is uncomfortable as hell, and she's my cousin, and...ugh, they're really getting into it now."

"I think it's sweet," I tell him.

"Do you two need to get a room?" Andrew asks loudly.

Tess pulls back immediately, looking at a very dazed Mouse. "Don't get any ideas," she warns him sharply. "This is a one-time thing because you're definitely not it for me."

"Okay," Mouse says, blinking a few times. "Th-thank you."

"You're welcome," she says, then turns to all of us. "Whose turn is it now?"

"I'm getting all pruney," Beau complains, holding up both hands.

"And I don't think anything is going to top what we've witnessed here," Andrew says.

Somehow, the bottle of vodka has made it into my hands, so I take a swig.

"Andrew," I call, holding the bottle out for him. "You."

"Me," he says happily before gulping down the rest.

"Your house is massive, Mouse," Tess says. "You couldn't have gotten your parents to make the pool a little smaller to fit a hot tub?"

He laughs as he kicks his legs and spins himself around to face her. "There's a jacuzzi in one of the upstairs bathrooms."

"Let's go!" she squeals, attempting to sprint out of the water.

Mouse follows her out quickly, trailed by Beau.

"You coming?" Andrew asks me as he grips the edge.

I glance at Cole, who shakes his head.

"I think I'll pass on this one," I answer for the both of us.

He waggles his eyebrows at Cole, then pulls himself out of the pool. "Suit yourself."

When it's only the two of us left, I smile happily because even though we're in a different location, we've still managed to end up in the water and under the stars.

And there's still so much I want to know about him.

"Truth or dare?" I ask him, fluttering my fingertips over the surface.

"Truth."

"What was so embarrassing about the last game of Truth or Dare you played with Tess?"

Cole lets out an audible sigh. "You're horrible, you know that?"

"Rule of the game," I say simply. "You have to answer."

"She made me go streaking," he replies after a beat. "And then locked me out of the house."

I choke on a laugh.

"Go ahead," he sighs, shaking his head.

The full volume of my amusement escapes my throat. "Oh my god," I wheeze.

"She timed it perfectly. Uncle Kevin was just coming home from a shift, and you know how he is."

I howl at that mental picture, and he waits patiently for me to settle.

"No more games or stories about Tess torturing me," Cole scolds with a smirk when I'm able to breathe again. "I'm trying to impress you, not come off as an idiot."

I chuckle and swim closer. "I'm already very impressed, Cole."

"Well, that's good to know," he says, reaching for me.

I slide my hands around his neck, sensing the shift between us. "Do you want to float for a little while?"

He nods. "Yeah."

On instinct, I wrap my legs around his waist, but as our skin slides together, I'm aware of how intimate this position is.

The nervous energy that bubbles up in me at that realization makes me want to spring off him and hide my embarrassment under the water.

But the simultaneous charge of exhilaration keeps me grounded, and I lock my ankles firmly behind him as he pushes my hair back off my shoulders.

He skims his fingertips down my arms, connecting all the little sun freckles like he's creating his own constellations, and then he kisses me well into the night.

FIFTEEN

"I think this might be our best production yet," Joe says encouragingly.

I'm slightly out of breath after uttering the final words at our last dress rehearsal, relieved to be done talking and projecting my voice for the day.

"Really great energy today, everyone," he compliments. "It's hard to believe we're only a day away from showtime."

I can't believe it either, honestly.

Despite the grueling process of production, we've all established a sort of togetherness. The night in the pool bonded us in a way I couldn't have anticipated would help make the twelve-hour days even better.

We've rehearsed the same scenes and lines over again, and our little inside jokes are a comfort even when I don't think I can say Alice's lines one more time.

The time spent in the theater is fantastic for the relationship-building of our core group, but they've all, unknowingly, helped me avoid the continued shattering of my parents' relationship.

Because now that my parents' secret is out to me, they're less careful about hiding their little arguments.

And the fact that my dad sleeps on the couch.

My parents only seem capable of forming a united front when they want to talk about me, the play, or the fall semester ahead—the inevitable future that's waiting for me at the end of August, just a few weeks away.

I, for one, am pretending that a roommate, a meal plan, and unfamiliar classrooms aren't looming ahead of me. It's not that I'm not looking forward to college, per se, but I just feel so lukewarm about the entire experience that—

A shove of my shoulder jolts me out of my thoughts, and I blink in time to see Esme pass by in irritation.

I chuckle quietly at her unspoken attitude as I make my way to the dressing room.

With all the changes happening in my life, I'm almost relieved I can count on her to maintain her same unforgiving presence.

After pulling back on my regular clothes and hanging Alice's gown on the rack, I drop down in front of one of the lighted mirrors. I wonder if it's even worth attempting to wipe off the heavy stage makeup now or if I should just deal with it later in the shower.

"You know why she doesn't like you, right?" Andrew leans against the counter, his tone curious rather than cruel.

"Esme?" I clarify, slumping back in the chair.

He nods. "Yeah."

"To be honest, before this summer, I didn't even think she knew who I was. Now, after all this time, I've landed on it being something between jealousy and a general resentment for my existence."

He laughs. "You nailed it. But I'm glad to see you're not upset about it."

"I don't see a point," I admit.

"I do," Andrew scoffs. "I can't imagine being one of those people who just goes around being generally unliked."

"You're just *so* popular," I tease. "It's impossible for anyone to not like you."

He pretends to toss a lock of hair over his shoulder as he smiles and tilts his head from side to side. "I know."

I snort and shake my head. "There was a time in my life I never put thought into making friends or worrying about whether people liked me."

"Even with all the things people say online about you and *Wanda*?" Andrew asks.

"It wasn't a concern until I transferred schools last year, and I found out that a lot of people were more like Esme than my old friends. But I guess that's part of life, right? You leave the comforts you've grown up in just to have to figure it all out again."

"Or maybe we are just doomed to repeat high school dynamics over and over again," he proposes. "High school, college, jobs, any sort of group gathering…"

"Thanks for the reassurance," I deadpan.

"Whatever the future holds," Andrew says, softening. "I'm just glad I got to meet you."

I smile at him. "Same."

"Especially when all of Joe's industry friends see you in this role," he continues. "I mean, I can tell people in ten years that I was there when your career took off again."

"Stop." I roll my eyes. "No such thing is going to happen."

"Are you kidding me?" He furrows his brow. "There's no chance you'll walk out of here tomorrow night without shaking the hand of some big fancy person."

I frown at the thought, especially juxtaposed with the conversation I overheard between Joe and Esme at the beginning of the summer.

Because this show isn't about me—it's about the entire cast, the crew, the writers.

"But, hey, no pressure, right?" Andrew adds.

"Right," I say half-heartedly, letting myself consider the idea that something really big might come from this.

And it's terrifying.

The idea of acting for a living, finding myself in other characters and exploring their lives, is something I haven't allowed myself to consider. I've been too focused on this play and this summer with Cole to really open myself up to anything else.

I've already known fame, and from what I've seen, it's only gotten more intense in my absence.

Falling in love with performing again has been almost seamless, but I haven't actually made it to the actual show to prove to myself I can do it again.

Because rehearsals and memorization are one thing, but actually putting myself out there in front of an audience…

I get a little nauseated just thinking about it.

And that, obviously, isn't good.

"Hey," Cole says as he appears at the dressing room door.

"Hey," I return, both grateful for the interruption and his presence.

"Can I steal you for a bit?" he asks me.

"I'd hardly call it 'stealing,'" Andrew says with a grin, then he turns to me. "I'll see you tomorrow, yeah?"

"Yeah," I say, feigning enthusiasm despite my nerves. "Big day and all."

Cole reaches for my hand, and we walk in silence toward my car.

"Where's Tess?" I ask as I slide in the driver's side.

"Mouse is driving her home," he replies with a smirk.

I blink. "And that means…?"

"She's doing me a huge favor so you and I can have some time alone."

My smile widens. "And what price did you have to pay for that?"

"I'm sure I'll find out eventually," Cole laughs.

"Well, thank you for that," I say, moving to put the car in drive.

"Hang on a second," Cole says in a rush, reaching behind him. "I have something for you."

"You got me something?"

"Well, I made it, but yeah."

He pulls out a parcel made of spare fabric.

I eye it curiously. "Isn't *your* birthday sooner than mine?"

"Just open it," he says as he hands it over.

I smile as I struggle to untwist and make my way through the layers of cloth.

After unwrapping what feels like thirty pieces of fabric, I hold up a wooden box that's so big, I have to cradle it in both hands. The exterior is smooth, even though it's assembled from several different-sized pieces of scrap wood, and it's been stained a beautiful rich brown color.

"With us moving into maintenance and repair mode instead of outright building set pieces, Craig offered to show us the kind of stuff he makes in his shop," Cole explains.

"This is beautiful," I tell him, running my thumbs along the smooth edge.

"If someone told me months ago that I would be spending the summer in Pennsylvania inhaling sawdust, I would have laughed in their face. But yeah, Craig has been helping me learn more about this kind of stuff, and I really like it. I did every step for this myself. Sanding, priming, staining, picking out the finish. Open it up."

I flip it open and gasp.

A few broken mirror fragments are glued inside the top in a way that makes it look like a mosaic. There are hooks on the inside, and in the deepest part toward the bottom, there are several pieces of wood that serve as separators.

"You like jewelry," Cole explains. "But I noticed in your room that all your pieces were mixed together in that container, so I thought maybe you'd like something more official and organized."

I smile, already imagining how I'll arrange my items in this little Cole Keller original.

"Thank you," I say, leaning over to kiss him. "This is so beyond thoughtful."

"I try," he says nonchalantly.

I place the box gently on the backseat, resisting the urge to buckle it in. "Want to go somewhere?"

He nods. "Anywhere as long as you're there."

"So romantic," I say softly.

"What do you have in mind?" Cole asks.

I exhale. "Obviously the most fabulous place on Earth."

He playfully glares at me. "You're taking me to Sheetz again, aren't you?"

"Yes," I say with a laugh.

"Of course."

We drive all the way there with our fingers threaded together.

I'm almost reluctant to drop our grasp to fuel up, but once I've got a full tank—and a bag of candy to keep us going—we pick right back up where we left off.

At first, I drive us around a little aimlessly, trying to decide where we can go.

Cole seems content to hold my hand and watch out the window, which brings me an immeasurable amount of peace.

With all the uncertain thoughts swirling in my head, it's comforting to just *be* with him.

He's the only person who makes me feel like I do when I'm floating among the stars, like he's my own personal sky, there for me to admire and imagine that I'm a part of, a constant among the chaos.

I wonder if there's just magic in our proximity, him living next door, or if we'll do just fine in other settings.

On a whim, I veer to move onto the interstate, feeling my heart pound as I look at the directional signs and press my foot on the gas.

"Feeling like a road trip?" Cole asks casually.

"Just about an hour drive," I answer. "If you're up for it?"

"Definitely." He settles deeper into his seat, pulls out a phone I haven't seen, and turns on some music at a low volume.

"Is that new?" I ask, looking at the iPhone that's a few generations newer than mine.

"I think Aunt Marlene felt bad for me," he says sheepishly before popping a piece of gum into his mouth. "So yeah, I'm back in this decade, which is nice."

"And have there been any interesting developments?"

"I've gotten a few texts and calls from people in New York. Random people I went to school with who want me to go visit them or who are calling just to brag about their own trips. The person I've heard from the most, though, is Daniel. He's been begging me to come back."

"Do you think you will?" I force my tone to remain neutral. "Go back, I mean?"

Cole takes a beat to blow a bubble and crackle his gum between his teeth. "I've been thinking about what to do. I mean, the lawyer told Aunt Marlene that there's no chance in hell my dad will get off with anything less than ten years in prison. And all the accounts are still frozen."

"There's nothing they can do for you?" I frown. "I mean, surely someone understands that even though he did...what he did, *you* still have to continue on."

He shrugs. "I have a savings account that's all mine, but it'll barely pay for one semester of college."

A pang of guilt surfaces at how privileged I am.

I'm facing automatic admission and free tuition, and yet I've been considering tossing it aside for something as selfish as my own desire.

"Honestly, the more I think about it, the less I actually want to go to school," he continues. "Not just at Yale, but anywhere. For now, at least. My identity has been tied to my family's for so long that I've never stopped to think about what *I* want to do. I was so focused on what my father wanted that now that he's incarcerated, I'm kind of at a loss. Is that ridiculous?"

"No," I say forcefully. "Not at all."

"What about you?" Cole asks, clearly directing the conversation away from him. "Have you picked a major yet? Or started scoping out decor for your dorm room?"

I grimace at the prospect. "I have my class schedule all set," I offer instead.

"Oh really? What are you taking?"

"Some basic classes." I hand over my phone. "It's in my starred email folder if you're interested."

"The ultimate sign of trust," Cole says, tapping then swiping.

I steal a brief glance at him. "Showing you my class schedule?"

"Handing over your phone. I mean, even Daniel has never handed over his unlocked phone without watching me like a hawk."

"I trust you," I tell him.

Cole grins. "Good to know. Okay, let's see here. History.

Writing. Psychology. Nice. Well, all these classes seem kind of interesting."

"If by 'interesting,' you mean 'boring,' then yes," I retort.

"Don't say that. Your schedule will hear you," Cole mock-scolds, pretending to cover the phone's nonexistent ears.

I sigh and grumble, "Sorry, schedule."

Our conversation peters out in favor of listening to music on Cole's new phone.

It gives me plenty of time to let the words we've exchanged sink in and the truths behind them to surface.

I get a little jittery as I take the exit toward my old town, taking back roads and routes that only locals know, as I consider what I want to see.

Originally, I thought it'd be nice to show Cole the lovely two-story Tudor I grew up in, revealing another part of myself in a way. I wanted to see Cole juxtaposed against my old life, but now, it seems useless to do so.

It's not that it will be painful to drive by the structure that holds so many good memories, but more that I'm determined to come to terms with something that sprang up in my conversation with Andrew.

It's completely dark out by the time we come to a stop in front of an old drive-in theater.

It's been shut down for many years—and by all accounts left to rot.

The gate is rusty and permanently fixed closed with a deadlock, and the once-pristine grass and gravel property is now overgrown. It has kind of a post-apocalyptic feel to it, but I don't hesitate to pull over.

I jump out of the car, grateful that the streetlights are still illuminated in this part of town. I have just enough light to identify a gap in the fence behind a few half-dead bushes.

"Breaking and entering?" Cole asks, voice light as he follows me.

"I've had some practice lately," I tease.

He smirks and holds back the chain-link as I crawl through it, then he follows me inside.

It's a little eerie to be in a place that's been abandoned, but I continue forward without hesitation, walking purposefully around the ticket booth and old concession stand.

"You know, I've never been to a drive-in movie before, but I think you're supposed to stay in the car," Cole says wryly.

"You've never been?" I sigh. "You city kids are really neglected."

He chuckles as I reach for his hand, pulling him along and over to what I want to show him.

"Here," I say, gesturing to the wall.

"A *Wanda* poster?" Cole says, a little confused as he takes it in.

The picture of me is preserved within a very dirty glass case. I can tell from where I stand that the white of the paper edge has yellowed over time.

But it's still the same old me I've seen online and reflected back at me in the mirror my entire life.

I step forward, getting a closer look at the image and smile as I recall when it was taken.

It was a very long day of meetings, discussing a range of

topics such as contracts, my "brand," my interview style, and it was all a little demoralizing.

The studio's hot lights beamed down on me while the photographer gave me cues and my mom stood behind the camera, trying to make me relax and laugh into getting the perfect shot.

I look joyful and innocent in this photo, smiling widely as a purple light of magic—digitally added in later—radiates from my fingertips.

But I frown at it now.

I wish I could go back in time and hug my younger self before all the embarrassment and hardship occurs. Then again, I'm not sure what words of comfort I could offer because years have passed and I still don't think I've overcome what unfolded.

I love performing because it allows me to get lost in myself, to play pretend that I'm someone else. I'm able to funnel my emotions through characters and costumes and escape reality.

I'm aware, though, if I want to do that all over again, I have to put myself out there and endure even more pressure and ridicule.

And I'm not sure if that reality is worth playing pretend for a living.

"Alexandra," Cole prods softly, watching me trace the outline of my own face. "Do you want to do this again? Acting? Like for a living? Instead of going to school in the fall?"

"I don't honestly know." I turn and look at him, my vision slightly blurred with tears. "And it's a little terrifying."

"It's okay," he says, pulling me into his arms.

"I don't know what I want," I admit, pressing my whole self against him. "Other than you."

I feel the rumble of laughter in his chest before he drops a kiss on top of my head, making me not ever want to let him go.

SIXTEEN

I'm flawless as Alice.

On the outside, at least.

My costume is freshly steamed and pristine. My hair is held in place with at least a pound of hairspray. My makeup is heavily exaggerated for the audience's benefit—no one wants a washed-out main character.

My preparations go even deeper than looks, though.

I doubt I'll forget my lines for the rest of my life, and I definitely could walk out on that stage right now and perform with my eyes closed.

I feel ready, but it doesn't stop the nerves.

The audience of our sold-out show slowly files into their assigned seats. The auditorium that once seemed so cavernous gradually shrinks, and the happy sound of excited chatter reverberates off the walls.

And all the while, I bite my nails in the wings of the stage, completely destroying my manicure.

From what I recall during my film and television work,

we had an insane number of takes, even after multiple readings and rehearsals. If I stepped on a costar's line or misspoke during one of my own, it was fine because that scene could easily be cut or reshot.

This, however, is a one-night-only live show.

The pressure is on, and I can feel the weight of it threatening to buckle my knees. I'm breathing slowly, in and out, as if that will stop the thudding in my chest and the pit from growing in my stomach.

It doesn't help that I'm still a little emotionally raw from last night's impromptu road trip with Cole. His reassurance was exactly what I needed then, but now, I'm not sure what will help.

"Alexandra," Esme hisses as she approaches.

She looks at me without revealing a single emotion on her face, and I'm a little elated that anger, irritation, and frustration overtake the worry that seemed so daunting a second ago.

I doubt she's here to give me a pep talk, but I know even though I'm given a brief reprieve from having a mental freak-out, I absolutely don't think it's a good idea to expend the energy required to deal with her attitude before the curtain rises.

"Not now, Esme," I say sharply.

"Ah, a backbone finally forms without Tess around," she sneers, her hands on her hips.

"Go away, Esme. Can't you find someone else to make feel inferior for just one night?"

She purses her lips. "I deserve that."

I blink and refocus. "What?"

Esme peeks out through the curtain, studies the audience with a frown, then snaps her gaze back to mine.

I try to stop my fidgeting, but I'm not in control of it at this moment.

And Esme, of course, notices.

"Whenever I'm nervous, I hold something small, like a spare button or a bobby pin, and I try to visualize channeling all my nervous energy into it. Then I hide it on my costume or in my hair and let it soak up all my doubts as I step on stage." She pauses and clucks her tongue. "Sounds kind of stupid when I say it aloud, but it works."

"You're...helping me?" I ask in disbelief. "Why?"

She sighs. "Call it a moment of temporary insanity."

"Or sheer human decency?" I suggest.

"Or the fact that Tess may or may not have just threatened my life because she's a little concerned you're going to repeat history by fainting."

I can't help but snort as I catch sight of my neighbor across the stage, headset on and body hunched over the soundboard. "And you went along with it?"

"She thought you could use some advice," Esme says with a shrug. "And look, I mean, I've been thinking about what she said at the party, anyway. The way I look at it, you and I are the same, Alexandra."

I don't have a response for that.

At my silence, she elaborates. "We're both coming from this stupid school and town, and we're bigger than it. Or we're going to be. I mean, you already are, but you seem like you're too scared to go for it."

That sentence is like a slap in the face, but it's the truth.

I didn't even have to dare her to say what I've been too afraid to admit to anyone, even Cole.

"The industry is big enough for both of us," Esme finishes. "Might as well not start off with any enemies as we both go for it."

I suck in my bottom lip, likely ruining my lipstick. "I'm not even sure I am going to be in the industry again."

"Scared," she huffs, challenging me again before glancing out into the theater once more. "You have every reason to be, but from what I hear, the big risks bring even better rewards."

I open and close my mouth a few times, stunned by the turn of this conversation.

"It's not just Joe's industry friends who are here," Esme tells me. "There's also going to be a model scout and a talent agent."

I feel my forehead crease in confusion. "Okay."

"So I'm going to play the sexiest, boldest queen I possibly can." She turns to face me full-on, staring me down. "And you're going to absolutely crush it as Alice, you understand?"

I nod, somewhat shocked into silence.

"Good." She flips her hair over her shoulder. "Well, it's probably time for me to do some touch-ups."

"Okay," I say, exhaling the weight of the expectations I've been dragging around.

With her long, perfectly unchewed fingernails, she yanks a bobby pin out from the top of her hairdo and holds it out to me. "Here."

I extend my hand, accepting the little twist of metal in the palm. "Thanks," I say with a tight smile.

After a final nod, she retreats, staring Tess down as she moves toward me.

"Was that as...pleasant as it looked?" Tess asks as she approaches. "It was hard to tell from where I stood."

"It wasn't the worst," I answer. "It actually helped. I think, so thanks for intervening."

"You've got five minutes until curtain," she tells me. "Better get in place."

I nod, then move to the center of the stage, toes square in the middle of my mark—the little X marked on the floor in tape.

I take a deep, calming inhale before I take Esme's advice.

It's almost too easy to channel all my nervous energy into the bobby pin. I think about all the jitters, from my shaking legs all the way up to the tremor in my hands, even pulling back into the memories of that fateful award show.

In its place, I project what ideally I'd like to have for this performance and give myself some compliments and encouragement.

Once I finish, I stick it in the back of my own hair—keeping it close as a reminder, but allowing myself to move forward.

I can do this, I decide.

The adrenaline hits when the curtain rises.

There's no Andrew, Mouse, Beau, Esme, Aggie, or me for the next hour and a half—it's only our characters, their conversations, and their lives. They've been real to us all this time, but now we get to help the audience believe.

The scenes and lines are a blur, but I execute each line and motion perfectly.

I'm happy to give myself over to Alice's world, finding it thrilling, rewarding, and exhilarating all at once.

But it's over far, far too soon.

I don't get to mourn the loss of it, though, because suddenly, Andrew and Mouse link arms with me.

We're supposed to be silent as we line up on stage and wait to take our bows, like we're surprising the audience with our presence.

But we don't bother following the norm, choosing instead to let it all out. Just like when we won Flip Cup, we celebrate with laughter and screams.

The smile doesn't fall from my face as the audience gives us a standing ovation, and I have to blink back the rush of elation.

I've never been so certain that I was made for anything in this world as much as I am this feeling.

After the curtain drops for the final time, we all rush to change out of our costumes and into our street clothes. I don't bother wiping off my heavy stage makeup before I head into the lobby. I accept flowers and a kiss from Cole, then the same from my parents, along with a hug from Marlene and a handshake from Mr. Keller.

They all gush over the performance, and while I appreciate the support, I don't think any of their comments, good or bad, will change anything.

Maybe, I realize, that's what every single actor feels. That it's all about what's inside, and all the noise they have to endure outside of performing is worth it.

I try to take it all in, cataloging this power inside me and memorizing as many details as possible as I scan the room.

Beau, Mouse, and Andrew are all in a group with their parents, receiving hugs and congratulations, just like I did. I briefly notice Esme getting chatted up and introduced to people by Joe.

Then I blink and catch a distantly familiar face heading toward me.

Even though I haven't seen her in a decade, I easily pick my old acting coach out of the crowd.

"Rachelle?" I say with surprise.

My parents turn abruptly at that name, startled as she brings me in for a hug.

"What are you doing here?" I ask.

Rachelle laughs as she pulls back. "When I heard through the grapevine that my little star was getting back into showbiz, I had to come see it for myself," she says in her distinctive, raspy voice.

"This was just a one-night thing," I say, setting her expectations if she wasn't aware of it already.

"The show's over," she agrees. "But I know you felt it."

"Felt what?"

"The high, Alexandra, like you're on another level of consciousness."

The words roll from her mouth easily, but their honesty nearly breaks my chest open.

I'd almost welcome it, choosing to bare my soul to the world in exchange for living in this forever.

"Rachelle, it's good to see you," my mom says with a smile.

"You too," Rachelle says, greeting both my parents with a handshake.

My dad nods. "Such a trip to see you after all these years."

"It is," she agrees before turning her attention back to me. "You graduated high school this spring, right?"

"She's going to the university downtown this fall," he answers for me.

If Rachelle didn't have an obscene amount of Botox in her forehead, I'm betting it would crease at this admission. "Studying theater?"

I shake my head. "Undeclared major."

"Oh, really?" She taps her purse twice, like she's cataloging this information. "Can you do lunch on Monday?"

"Sure," I agree immediately. "It would be great to catch up."

My parents are pulled into a conversation with the Kellers, and Rachelle takes the opportunity to lower her tone.

"There's actually someone I would really like you to meet." She smiles a little devilishly. "I'll send the details to your mom. Her email address still the same as before?"

I nod. "Yes."

"Great," she says. "I'll see you then."

When she leaves, Cole approaches. "Who was that?"

"My past," I say, watching her walk away. "And maybe my future."

SEVENTEEN

The awkwardness in the car Monday afternoon is palpable.

Compared to the elation and bliss of Saturday night, this feels stifling.

I've already crashed and burned from that post-show high—a decline that not even an elongated float session in the pool with Cole yesterday could cure.

I'm trying to be mature and rational about the divorce, but it's almost comical how my whole family is clearly at a loss as to how to interact around one another at this point.

If my parents hadn't told me, would we all be at ease, talking easily about all the things we used to tease and chat about?

I'm having a hard time wrapping my head around how they buried their true feelings for so long, only for one little sentence to change everything. It's not lost on me that I've just stumbled across the reason why I am the way I am, playing pretend to avoid reality.

Still, I'm relieved when we enter the restaurant and are

forced to share space with a dozen or so other tables who all have their own lives and sets of problems. That somehow makes mine feel less devastating.

After all, no human on Earth is having a perfect existence, and while my problems are my entire world, they're much better than what others have to deal with. Compared to hunger, starvation, or war, my worries about the future seem embarrassingly selfish.

"Over here, Alexandra," Rachelle calls.

I plaster a smile on my face as my parents trail behind me, and we approach the table where my former acting coach sits, joined by an unfamiliar woman.

"Thank you so much for coming," Rachelle says after a few brief hugs. "This is Stacy Kimball, my longtime friend and a professor at Juilliard."

I force myself not to gasp.

The Juilliard School in New York is about as prestigious a performing arts school as they come. The list of notable playwrights, dancers, and performers that have gotten their start there is so long, I can't even pick out an example off the top of my head.

A few years ago, back when college conversations were beginning at school, I looked up Juilliard's admission requirements on a whim, then balked at the cost and resigned to never consider it again.

I glance at my mother, who received the details of our reservation, to see if she knew what I was in for.

Judging by her wide eyes, she was left in the dark as well.

"It's nice to meet you," I manage.

"You as well," Stacy returns kindly.

"Nice to meet a fellow professor," my dad effuses as we all sit down.

Stacy nods. "Yes, yes, I heard that."

"Alexandra is going to attend fall term at the university where he's teaching," Rachelle explains, glancing at my mother, who corroborates the story with a nod.

"Rachelle tells me you're not studying anything related to drama?" Stacy cuts right to the point.

"Correct," I say before taking a sip of water.

"Allie hadn't even given us an inkling she was interested in performing again before this summer," my dad explains.

"But, of course, we're thrilled for whatever path she takes," my mom adds. "And we'll try to support her as best we can."

I get déjà vu about their united front, their ability to put aside their issues as long as they can focus on me, and it's not the best feeling in the world.

I barely shake off my discomfort as the server approaches.

We all place our brunch orders, and while the adults stick with coffee and healthier food options, chocolate chip pancakes remain my go-to. I feel a little juvenile ordering them—and in front of a representative from Juilliard, no less—but, of course, I still do.

"I'm so disappointed I couldn't see your show," Stacy laments to me after a bit of small talk about her trip down here. "Rachelle tells me it was fantastic."

"Truly," Rachelle says, beaming. "I thought the play itself was an interesting spin on a classic story, but the way you brought Alice to life, Alexandra, was magnificent. The rawness, the dark humor, the emotion...it was beautifully done. If I didn't know otherwise, I would never guess you've taken all this time off from acting."

"You haven't done any production at all?" Stacy asks.

I shake my head as our server reappears to drop off their mugs of steaming hot coffee. "After *Wanda,* I only did a few gigs before I…quit permanently, and then last year, I worked as a crewmember on my school's fall play and had a small part in the spring one."

"Wow," she breathes. "And still, Joe thought you had the chops to carry the production in the lead role."

"You know Joe?" my mom asks.

A ghost of a smile forms on Stacy's face. "We…go back a few years. Dated while he lived in New York and have stayed in touch here and there."

"Oh," I say, wondering if I've earned his attention for the wrong reason.

"He's actually the reason I'm in town," she continues. "We've been trying to get him to return to New York and take on a professorship, but he seems reluctant to leave his hometown again."

"I can definitely see the appeal," Rachelle admits as our food arrives. "But there's something about New York I don't think I'll ever be able to leave behind."

"Especially in the fall," Stacy agrees. "And the campus is beautiful."

"Are you spending a lot of time there now?" my mom asks Rachelle. "What about LA?"

"I'm bicoastal," she explains. "These days, I have just as many clients on Broadway as I do on-set in California, and with more actors splitting their time between both locations, it just makes sense."

Stacy takes a sip of coffee, then smiles. "And that is a great segue into why I was so happy Rachelle wanted to make an introduction."

My grip on my fork tightens as I sit frozen, waiting for her next words.

"This conversation comes too late for the fall semester, and we're cutting it close even for spring, but there's a round of open auditions for Juilliard's drama program this week. I think you should consider attending."

My heart thuds in my chest.

"Your Alice monologue from the second act would be perfect for it," Rachelle adds before taking a bite.

Stacy purses her lips. "I wish I could personally vouch for you for a private audition, but I'm sure you can understand my hesitancy, given that I haven't seen you in action myself aside from your role in *Wanda*. However, I can say that this would be a great opportunity if you're seriously considering restarting your career and college is on your must-do list."

I can practically feel my parents seize up in panic at the sudden change in plans.

"Oh, wow," my mom says, after a few blinks, voice a little shaky. "That's...a big deal. College in New York."

My dad smiles tightly as he looks to me. "Is this something you'd want to consider?"

From their reaction, I gather they don't love the idea.

To be honest, I'm not sure how I feel about it either. Not only would I be leaving the safety net of my home state but I'd be taking on a mountain of debt in lieu of getting a free ride at my dad's university.

Still, I close my eyes, briefly imagining myself exploring New York and learning from the greats at Juilliard.

To even stand in a room where creativity is the main currency…

There's no way I can't *not* go for the audition.

Even if nothing comes of it—which I don't believe it will—it doesn't hurt to try. If I don't, I know I'll regret it for the rest of my life.

"I think I would like to go," I say as confidently as I can.

Rachelle's lips quirk up. "I was hoping you'd say that. Stacy already sent me the details, so I'll forward those along to you momentarily. All you have to do is show up and bring the same passion and energy you did on Saturday, and you'll be a shoo-in, I'm sure."

I grin back as the server drops off our check. "I can't thank—"

"We'll have to discuss this when we get home," my dad interjects firmly as he fishes out cash from his wallet to settle the bill. "There's a lot to consider."

"There is, but I'll be there," I tell both Rachelle and Stacy.

"We'll see," my mom adds as she stands.

The irritation at my parents that I pushed down when we first arrived crawls to the forefront of my mind, and I barely hold it in as we say our goodbyes to Rachelle and Stacy.

Once we're in the car again, the silent standoff resumes, and I try to plan exactly what to say to them as we make our way home.

"So, I'm going to go," I tell them as seriously as I can.

My mom clears her throat. "It's all very sudden. I didn't

even really think you were even remotely considering this. After all, when I suggested you audition in the fall for local programs, you seemed so disinterested."

"I know, and I agree," I say, acknowledging her concern. "Still, though, I want to go for it."

She grimaces, glancing over her shoulder at me in the backseat. "I get that, but going all the way up to New York this week? It's not a lot of notice."

"We're both in crunch time right now with work," my dad chimes in.

"I am eighteen," I remind them. "Old enough to go on my own."

I'm surprised by the forcefulness of my own declaration.

I chalk it up to a culmination of Tess rubbing off on me and my inner confidence rebuilding over the course of this summer.

Unfortunately, my mom is unfazed by my bravado.

"All by yourself in New York City for the first time?" She shakes her head. "I'm not sure that's the best idea."

"Why not?" I demand. "I'm perfectly capable of taking care of myself."

"I think the root of the issue is that, while this is great, it's all very sudden," my dad says as we turn at a light. "Months ago, you were set on going to the university. And now, you've gone from not even being interested in acting to wanting to put your hopes and dreams on a college that we don't even know we can afford."

I sigh. "I wouldn't be the first person to have to take out student loans. And I mean, I know you did some gigantic favor of moving here and taking that job so I could have free college, but you didn't even consult me! You were all set to make that big life decision without my consent, but somehow, this seems out of reach?"

"That's not exactly why we moved here," my dad grits out, giving me a quick reminder of the state of my parents' relationship.

"But this is a big leap from home," my mom presses.

"So what's going to happen next?" I argue. "You two divorce, I live in the dorms year-round, and we split Christmas between wherever you're going to live? Why does it matter if I live here or in a different state?"

"Allie," my mom starts.

But I don't let her continue. "How can you guys sit here and act normal? This isn't normal! And it's the first thing I have ever asked of you. Ever."

They exchange a look, and I can tell I haven't persuaded them yet.

I sigh and try again. "I don't even know if I'm good enough to get in, or what I really want from all this. But I know if I don't at least go for it, I'm going to hate myself for the rest of my life. Just like how you guys wanted a change of location to see if you could work things out. This is kind of like that for me."

Judging by the slight nod from my mother, she, at least, understands my need to go.

EIGHTEEN

The roar of the bus engine and the overpowering scent of gasoline aren't exactly comforting. But if I have any chance of making it in New York, I have to get used to the noise.

At least, that's what Cole says.

"You kids be safe," Marlene calls to us as we step up to board. "Don't get in too much trouble."

"We won't," I promise, offering her a reassuring smile.

After the lunch with Stacy and Rachelle, I went over next door to fill Cole in, but I interrupted a cooking show marathon session the three Kellers were having. It worked out, though, because Marlene championed this entire ordeal with my parents.

For as much groaning as Tess has done about our early departure, I think she's just as excited as I am to go to New York.

Because, while I do have the pressure of the audition looming tomorrow, I am romanticizing the idea of escaping our town with Cole, even if it's just for a few days.

Tess is the compromise.

My parents regard her as a buffer or some sort of responsible presence, but *her* parents, apparently, know better.

"Especially you, Tess Marie," Marlene says, shaking her head.

My lips twitch in amusement as I consider the likelihood of that.

Tess rolls her eyes. "Bye, Mom. Don't miss me too much."

I take in the drab blue interior of the bus that's going to shuttle us across Pennsylvania and New Jersey, noting the heavy smell of antiseptic and several already sleeping passengers.

We move toward the back until Cole idles by a vacant row.

He tilts his head. "Want the window?"

"That would be great," I say, eagerly anticipating my first look at the skyline.

"Of course," he says as he takes the seat beside me.

"You guys are annoyingly cute," Tess says as she lays on the two seats across the aisle from us.

I've honestly been waiting for anyone other than Andrew to voice an opinion on all the...whatever this is between Cole and me.

But so far, aside from a few grins from Marlene and curious glances from my parents, I've got nothing.

Not that I'm looking for validation, of course, but I can't help it.

Tess kicks her feet up on one of the arm rests, trying to get comfortable. "Nothing more romantic than seeing New

York for the first time from a dirty bus window and surrounded by forty drooling strangers."

"I'm sure we'll survive," Cole says.

"Just wake me up when we get there," she says, then pulls down the hood on her sweatshirt, effectively blocking us out.

"Ready?" Cole asks me, laying his arm on my thigh and holding out his hand.

I take it easily and relax, letting our shoulders touch as I lean back in my seat. "Absolutely."

He smiles as the bus lurches forward, pulling out of the terminal and officially marking the start of our trip. It's about ten hours total, with a stop in Philadelphia along the way.

Marlene very kindly stopped at Sheetz before dropping us off, and one of the bags at our feet is totally stuffed with snacks and drinks—a must-have for any trip.

Even though the seats aren't that comfortable and the internet is spotty, the ride is still pleasant. Cole and I spend the entire time just enjoying being together.

At first, we stare out the window, pointing out various buildings and people, but as we progress through Pennsylvania, there's not much to entertain us. We move on to playing games on my phone, trying to beat the clock in a silly little word app.

When that gets annoying, we draw letters on each other's thighs and try to guess what the person is spelling out. It makes me squirm and giggle, which only encourages Cole further.

As we cross into New Jersey, we switch to listening to music. We start with the new Travis Young album but eventually work our way backward through the decades, taking turns picking out a song that we like and reading along with the lyrics.

Before I know it, I get my first glimpse at the Manhattan skyline.

It's early evening, so there's an interesting hue to the city, and from our vantage point, it's mesmerizing.

It's almost difficult to believe buildings this tall can exist at all, so when I learn that they were built on the middle of an island that was once nothing, it just adds to the magic.

The lights of the city flicker on while we're stalled in traffic, and I'm awed at the realization of how many people live, work, and vacation here. I'm glad Cole offered me the window seat because I'm glued to the view as we navigate the streets.

I take in as much as I can while he offers anecdotes of his experiences with the various restaurants and neighborhoods.

We finally park along a narrow street, and Cole stands and stretches, then holds a hand out for me to do the same.

I lean over and shake Tess's shoulder. "Time to wake up."

She shrugs me off, mumbling about still being asleep.

"Tess, come on," I say, sidestepping so that some of the people behind us can exit.

"Go away," she groans.

"Any ideas?" I ask Cole.

He smirks before springing into action.

In one smooth motion, he wrenches back her hood, then drops her duffel bag on her stomach.

Tess groans and sits upright, glaring up at us with sleep-laden eyes.

"Welcome to the Empire State," Cole says sardonically.

She lets out a long, loud yawn. "What a way to be welcomed."

Cole smirks. "I thought you'd appreciate the direct approach. Come on, let's get out of here."

We're weighed down by our bags as Cole leads us a few streets over, escaping the crowd of people just enough to hail one of the famous yellow cabs.

The ride to the hotel—uptown, Cole informs us—is mostly stop-and-go traffic, and I'm just as impressed by the building we finally stop outside of as I am by the city itself.

"This place is something else," I say, craning my neck to look up.

Cole glances around somewhat uneasily before leading us through a back entrance and knocking twice.

Tess and I exchange looks of confusion, but the black metal door opens suddenly, slamming against the beige exterior.

"Mr. Keller," a man wearing coveralls greets Cole. "You're early."

"We made good time," he answers a little shortly.

The guy smiles, deepening the wrinkles around his eyes. "Did you bring what I asked?"

Cole slides a wad of cash into his hand. "Thanks for doing this, Jerry."

"Anytime," he says, pocketing the money. "Just remember that if you get caught, I had nothing to do with this."

"Right," Cole agrees, adjusting the strap of his bag across his shoulder. "Do you have the elevator key for me?"

Jerry hands over a tiny silver key. "You're only staying a short while, right?"

"Yeah," Cole confirms. "I'll slide this under your office door when we leave."

"Right on," Jerry says.

Cole smiles at him tightly as we follow him down a dark and musty hallway.

"What is going on?" I ask him, picking up on his unease. "I thought you said you got a deal on a hotel."

"I lied," Cole says flatly, turning the lock and opening the service elevator doors.

Tess snorts as he pushes the button for the top floor. "Obviously."

"So, what is this?" I ask him.

"My place."

I gawk at him. "You *live* in this building?"

"I did. Well, before it got raided because of my dad's dealings and closed off."

"A nice upgrade from the basement," Tess snickers as the elevator doors open. "Mr. Penthouse Suite."

Cole grimaces and unlocks a second set of doors that are covered with yellow NO TRESPASSING! tape.

I gasp at the interior we step into because, even by New York's skewed standards, this place is massive.

There are marble floors, extravagant light fixtures, and furniture that looks way too nice to even entertain the idea of sitting on. Amid the luxury, I can see the pockets of disheveled mess where the authorities tore the place apart looking for information on Cole's dad.

He leads us down the hallway toward the kitchen, slamming the door closed on what appears to be a trashed office.

"I don't know what food is still here," Cole says apologetically as he opens the fridge.

Tess yawns and snatches the bag of Sheetz snacks. "I'm going to binge then pass out."

"You slept the entire way here," I say with disbelief.

She shrugs. "What room should I take?"

Cole points back in the direction we just came from. "Either of the guest rooms."

"Right, I forgot you have *multiple* guest rooms, you rich trash bag," she says as she walks away.

I sputter at her words before breaking into laughter, and Cole eventually joins in.

As the sound peters out, I do a spin, trying to capture all the little details and imagine what it was like to grow up here.

"This is really nice," I tell him.

That's an understatement, though.

This is probably the most beautifully decorated place I've ever been in. It's only enhanced by the views of the city outside the windows, though they're slightly obscured at the moment.

"Thanks," Cole murmurs.

"Even though we are actually breaking and entering," I say, partly terrified of that fact but also too caught up in the entire experience to be frazzled.

Cole clears his throat. "I would offer a tour, but we probably shouldn't turn on any of the lights in this room. I don't want anyone to know we're up here."

"Right," I say resolutely. "Can I at least see your room?"

He holds out his hand for me to take. "Sure."

We walk in silence until we stop in front of a plain, nondescript white door, which he pushes open a little unceremoniously.

"Oh wow," I breathe, immediately crossing the plush carpet so I can press my face up against the window.

The views from the kitchen and living area were nice, but the one here, in his room, is absolutely *incredible*.

"That's Central Park," he says quietly, pointing out the very obvious greenery that I can make out even at this time of night. "And there are a bunch of residential buildings. That's a hotel. And that building right there is where Daniel lives."

"Will I get to meet him?" I ask eagerly.

"No, he's in Germany right now," he answers a little sadly. "I don't think any of my friends...if we're even still that...are around."

I offer a small, sympathetic smile. "I'm sorry."

"It's fine," Cole says dismissively.

"You're allowed to be upset," I remind him.

"I appreciate that. But this trip isn't about me or my issues or my friends. You deserve to revel in the spotlight, Alexandra, and not be dragged down by my family's problems."

"What if we could work on both?" I ask after a minute.

He lets out a breath. "Let's just take it one Juilliard audition at a time, okay?"

I laugh and squint out the window. "We can't really see the stars, though."

"Light pollution's a bitch," Cole says. "Definitely one bad thing about being in the middle of Manhattan."

I turn away from the window to take in more of his space.

His bed is massive, probably king-size, and on his desk is a Mac computer and a large second monitor. There are two doors in addition to the one we entered through, leading to what I assume are a closet and a bathroom.

In short, his bedroom is almost as large as the second floor of our house.

"I can't believe you live here," I breathe.

He scoffs, but the sound is pained. "I don't anymore. Well, at least not right now."

"I'm so sorry," I say.

He shakes his head, then swallows. "How are you feeling about your audition tomorrow?"

I sit down on the edge of the bed, which might just be the softest thing I've ever felt. "Okay, actually. I think I'm a little numb and still trying to process that we're here. It just feels like there's so much possibility around us, and I've barely seen any of the city."

"I've always been comforted by the fact that the city feels alive in its own way," Cole explains as he sits beside me. "Like just because I've stopped moving for a bit, New York continues on and is resilient on my behalf."

I squeeze his hand. "I can't even imagine what it was like growing up here, but I think I'd probably appreciate the experience more now. I can really see it, though. Rubbing elbows with the Wall Street types, running from audition to audition, and trying not to get lost on the subway."

Cole smiles and drops a kiss on my lips. "I can see it, too."

"Well, you should," I tease. "After all, you promised you'd be a taste-tester for my fabulous, late-night bakery. Where was it again? The Village or the Upper West Side?"

He drags his thumb under my bottom lip, eyeing me with a look of intensity. "I don't remember."

"Don't you want to play pretend?" I ask playfully.

He shakes his head, expression remaining serious. "I can't anymore."

My breath catches in my chest at the change in tone. "Why not?"

"This just feels too real, too much, too good," he says quietly, smile slowly forming.

And he's right.

It does.

Because as his lips crash down onto mine, I know that my reality is far better than anything I could even begin to dream up.

NINETEEN

If I were to take in the space through half-squinted eyes, I might be able to convince myself I'm in the theater back home. Even though this cavernous place is intimidating, the familiarity of just being in the presence of a stage is a comfort.

That realization is a little jarring.

It's taken some time, but looking at the stage is a welcome feeling, not a daunting one.

I walk down the long aisle, and each step I take reverberates up my body, jarring me in a way that keeps me on edge.

My nerves are mostly under control, but it doesn't help to see the three people sit at a table in front of the stage seem so poised and standoffish. As I approach, I smile at the group, but they all stare back completely stone-faced, giving me the impression I'm on trial.

I didn't think I'd miss Joe Morales's exaggerated personality, but I definitely prefer it now.

"Head to your mark and tell us your name, please," the person in the middle instructs, pointing toward the stage with the pen in his hand.

"Sure thing," I say clearly, then bound up the stairs.

The lights are low enough that I get a full view of all the empty seats, and I lean into that as a way to tell myself this isn't a big deal.

It's not like opening night, when hundreds of people were waiting to see me as Alice. It's just three strangers staring me down while they decide if I'm good enough to spend the next four years with them.

I swallow and step forward, projecting confidence. "I'm Alexandra Sutton."

"Alexandra Sutton," repeats the man who directed me up here. "What will you be auditioning with today?"

"I'll be performing a monologue from *In Wonder*," I tell the three of them. "It's a spin on *Alice in Wonderland* that I performed this summer with Joe Morales's local theater company in Pittsburgh."

I don't get any signs of recognition or interest.

"Go ahead, then," he says.

And so I do.

I repeat the same words I recited to get cast in *In Wonder*, but after so much time spent working on my diction and rhythm, it's even better than it was back then. My passion reignites for the monologue I'd been so sick of, and I lose myself once more in Alice's words and problems and character.

After a few minutes, as I come back down from the high of playing pretend, and the fog clears, I gradually register the ringing sound of silence.

I blink and clear my throat to compose myself.

"And why do you want to go to Juilliard?" The question comes from a woman with bright blonde hair and black horn-rimmed glasses.

My stomach sinks at the condescension in her tone, but just like I did moments ago, I force myself to believe that I belong with these people.

In truth, we're all just humans...even if they are more successful in their craft and careers than I am.

But I do recognize that even if I nailed my monologue, which I think I did, I still need to give a convincing reason why I belong here.

"I was a child star who had everything I dreamed of at that time. I got to grow up on movie sets and learn from seasoned actors. But for a number of reasons, I fell out of love with acting and put it aside for almost a decade...until this summer."

I pause to let those words sink in, for them and for me, and absorb the reminder of where I came from and just how much things have changed.

"The original part of Alice wasn't something I ever saw myself in. But she and I are the same. The adventures we've been on feel like a dream. She's given a choice of what path to take, but she's so caught up in the world that she doesn't even appreciate what she has."

I shift on my feet slightly as I continue.

"I feel the same way, and I feel like I've rediscovered a part of myself I didn't know was missing. While I do think I have the raw talent and passion for performing, I acknowledge that I need to grow and learn." Still getting no reaction, I lay it on a little thick. "And even auditioning before you has been incredible, and I'd be so grateful for your consideration to let me attend your school."

Again, I'm met with silence.

It's a loud one, during which my breathing is echoing in my ears so loudly, I fear it fills the entire room.

Finally, the third judge, a redheaded man, nods. "Thank you. I think that's all we need from you."

I smile tightly at the dismissal, trying to read anything from their body language or facial expressions but getting nothing.

It's not a great feeling.

But as I walk through the halls of the building toward the exit, I find I'm not devastated in the slightest.

Maybe it's because I'm not hinging the fate of my life on this step.

Maybe it's because this is just one of one million routes I can take in my future, like with Alice and her choices.

Or maybe it's because of the guy waiting for me outside, blowing a massive pink bubble and staring off into space.

"Hi," I say, catching his attention.

He jolts, then immediately pulls me in for a hug. "How'd it go?" Cole asks.

I fall into his arms and lay my head against his chest, feeling immediately comforted by his embrace. "Okay, I think."

"Okay?" Tess sneers.

I pull away from Cole's body slightly to meet his cousin's eyes.

"We rode in that boring, smelly bus all the way up here for you to do *okay*?"

"I don't know." I keep one arm wrapped around Cole's waist as he squeezes my shoulder reassuringly. "The people who were watching me were kind of hard to read, and I think I rambled a bit when they asked why I want to attend their school."

She rolls her eyes. "On your worst, most 'off' day, you're still a solid ten out of ten, Sutton."

"Thank you," I tell her, a little dumbfounded by her declaration.

"Whatever," Tess says flippantly. "Come on, there's a hot dog vendor around the corner, and I want to try one of those famous New York dogs. I only pray I don't get food poisoning."

"You know, they're actually really clean," Cole counters. "They have to pass all these inspections, and—"

"Cole?" a feminine voice calls just up ahead.

Cole's eyes widen at the smiling girl with bright yellow hair approaching us.

"Madison," Cole says, dropping his grasp on me so he can hug her fully. "What are you doing here?"

"I'm meeting Chris for lunch," she explains. "He's been interning at Dad's business all summer, so I've barely seen him."

"Who's Chris?" Tess asks, stepping forward to make her presence known.

Madison blinks at her, and then at me, appearing more outwardly surprised by the fact that Cole has people with him than she is that he's even here.

"Chris is my brother," she explains quickly. "Who are you?"

"I'm Tess," she says, extending her hand. "Cole's cousin."

Madison's cheeks warm as they shake briefly.

"And I'm Alexandra," I add with a smile.

"My girlfriend," Cole supplies, slinging his arm back around my shoulders.

"It's so nice to meet you," Madison says, trying to mask her surprise with politeness. "And it's especially good to see you again, Cole, after everything."

"You mean after my life imploded, and all my friends ditched me?"

I know how he feels, but I've never gotten to confront anyone head-on about it, so I merely squeeze his side in reassurance.

Madison shifts awkwardly. "It was…uh…you know investigators came by my dad's office, too? They wanted to see if there was any connection between him and your dad." She drops her gaze momentarily to the ground before she glances up again. "It's not like it was easy on all of us, wondering if our family members were going to be thrown in jail, or if we'd be kicked out of our homes."

"Uh-huh," Cole grits out, posture still rigid.

"Look," she says, softening. "I'm really sorry that we all pulled back. At least, I am. And it was a really shitty situation, but when all the dust started to settle after the verdict came down, I tried to reach out. A few of us did! Many, many times."

Cole exhales, unable to hold onto his irritation when she's being so genuine. "I appreciate that."

"I'd really love it if you came by my place on Friday,"

Madison says. "Everyone who's in town right now is coming over for a party, and it'll be really fun."

The mention of a large group, likely his former friends, causes his expression to sour.

"Can't," Cole says, forcing that same mask of indifference that I recognize from when we first met. "We have an overnight bus back to Pittsburgh in a few hours."

"Oh," Madison says, face falling slightly.

"So how do you two know each other?" Tess pipes up, pushing the awkward tension.

"We went to school together," Madison replies.

Tess eyes the other girl's ripped jeans and shredded band t-shirt. "*You* attended that fancy private school?"

Madison narrows her eyes playfully. "Should I be offended by that question?"

Tess laughs and shakes her head. "Not at all."

My jaw drops open because I don't think I've ever seen Tess smile, let alone show happiness.

Madison's phone buzzes in her pocket, and she pulls it out, frowning at the screen. "Well, Chris is waiting for me, so I'd better get going. Will you be back here soon, Cole?"

He shrugs. "Not sure yet."

"Okay," she says slowly. "Well, it was nice to meet you, Tess. Alexandra. I hope I'll see you all again."

"Me too," Tess says enthusiastically.

We start walking back up toward Cole's home, and Tess practically skips beside us.

"Hey, Cole?"

"Tess."

"That favor I wanted? The one I promised to cash in

someday after enduring close-quarters contact for an entire ride home with a boy who's now obsessed with me?"

Cole chuckles. "Sounds familiar, yes."

"Give Madison my phone number," Tess says slyly.

"Fine," Cole huffs as he pulls out his phone.

I smile as we continue on, and I try my best to memorize everything I'm experiencing now—the sounds of cars honking, the congestion on the sidewalks, the sense of belonging I feel in Cole's embrace.

As we walk, an ad on top of a cab catches my attention. It's not particularly flashy, but my eyes are drawn to the words "Acting & Film Academy." I mentally log the details and wonder if it's a fluke moment of serendipity or if I really am Alice, facing endless possibilities and adventures ahead.

TWENTY

The long bus ride back from New York segues into the laziest two weeks of summer yet.

With no rehearsals, no sets to build, and no behind-the-scenes coordination to take care of, Tess, Cole, and I fall into a little bit of a slump.

We spend our days alternating between binge-watching cooking shows and lounging by the pool, letting the rays soak into our skin.

I get more little constellations that Cole traces during our rare alone time when I sneak into the basement.

Tess spends an exorbitant amount of time on her phone, even when Mouse visits and practically pleads for attention.

Marlene is moderately entertained by our behavior, even going so far as to let Tess make us all margaritas one afternoon. After just one, I get a little giggly.

The respite is nice, a slow comedown from the show

and then impromptu trip to New York, but on the day of Cole's birthday, it all changes.

I walk into the kitchen, hair still dripping after an elongated afternoon pool session, to see my parents sitting at the table.

Part of this whole "enjoying the days of summer" has also meant "avoiding the impending break-up of my family," but I, apparently, have run out of time.

"Sit down, Allie," my mom says, although it sounds like more of a plea than an order.

I close my eyes and let out a breath before I do.

The divorce news rocked me, but I've had time to recover from the blow. This time, however, I'm approaching it with as cool of a head as I can.

But I have an inkling that this is one of those defining moments I'm going to remember for years to come.

"We have more news to share," my dad begins.

"Are you guys getting divorced again?" I ask with a little snark.

I've been spending far too much time with Tess for her attitude to not influence me, apparently.

But it does have the benefit of rousing a slight chuckle from my dad and a flat smile from my mom.

"Not exactly," she says. "But things are...moving along."

"I've found an apartment close to the university," my dad announces.

"Oh," is all I can say.

"With how competitive it is before the fall semester starts, I didn't expect anything to happen this fast." The details practically fall out of his mouth. "But if everything goes according to plan, I'll be there by the end of the month."

I swallow, giving myself a second to process this information.

The truth is, there are a number of ways I could play this.

I could funnel my anger into a snippy response, making fun of his "plan" to foray into bachelorhood. Alternatively, I could tap into my helplessness, beg him not to make such a drastic change merely weeks after dropping this on me.

But neither of those are exactly true, and I don't think now's the time to be inauthentic, even if it's my default to want to shy away.

I glance at their tentative expressions, both waiting for my response.

And for the first time, it saddens me that even though this life change affects them more than it does me, they're still stuck uniting as a force for my benefit.

I'm on the precipice of change, myself, but it's selfish to think that I'm the only one who needs to breathe and grow. They deserve to be happy and to find out what's next without worrying about how I feel about it.

"Okay," I say softly.

My mom blinks in surprise. "Okay?"

I nod and reach for her hand, trying to reassure her. "Where will *you* go, though?" I ask her.

"I'll stay here as we work out the house-selling process," she answers calmly. "With this market, it shouldn't be too long, and I can always stay at Marlene's if I need to."

I groan inwardly at the thought of my mom as Cole's new roommate.

Tess will be at culinary school, living in a shared apartment with three random girls, while I'll be in my university dorm with Ashley Jones, a transfer student from Indiana who seems nice enough via email.

"So, we're all changing locations, then?" I summarize with a sigh.

"Yes, we are," he says, letting out a breath that sounds suspiciously relieved.

I guess he thinks he's dodged some sort of emotional breakdown, and I suppose it's to their credit in how they raised me that I don't have one.

"Yours is the most exciting of all," my mom says warmly. "You're going to college! Wasn't Ashley going to email you with her thoughts on a preferred dorm layout?"

"Oh, yeah," I say, opening the email app on my phone to see if she responded.

My mom muses, "I was thinking it makes sense to do the stacked formation, so—"

She stops abruptly when she sees the expression on my face. "What happened?" she asks warily.

I hold up my phone with shaking hands. "It's from Juilliard."

They both lean forward in anticipation, eager for the news.

I swallow and reread the words before I open my mouth. "I didn't get in."

———

An hour later, after I've changed into dry clothes and primped, my parents and I walk into the Keller kitchen.

"Doesn't it look like a birthday cake threw up in here?" Tess asks us.

I take in the absurd number of streamers and balloons crowding the space. "Kind of," I admit.

"I didn't get to do anything for either of your birthdays," Marlene says defensively as she rearranges the freshly baked cupcakes on the counter. "So all this need to celebrate has just been building up. Besides, Cole's been through a lot these past few months, so I thought it would be nice to go all-out."

"I really appreciate it," he tells her kindly, appearing beside me. "But you didn't have to go through all the trouble."

Marlene snorts. "Trouble? You're an absolute angel compared to Tess."

"Hey now!" her daughter protests. "I didn't even get one detention last year."

"Because you sweet-talked your way out of every single one," I retort, recalling how impressive that process was to witness.

"Anyway," she says pointedly, pivoting the conversation. "Dinner's ready. Let's dig in!"

"It smells amazing in here," my dad says.

Tess opens the oven, letting the smell of hot dough, garlic, tomato sauce, and cheese fill the air. "I spent all day trying to make this freaking New York–style pizza."

Cole grins. "And I am forever grateful."

"It's tricky because it has to be thick enough to stay together when you fold it but thin enough that you can eat a massive slice without getting too full," Tess explains to my parents. "Cole gave Sutton and me a rundown before we boarded the bus back here."

"I'm sure that's a topic you'll become an expert in when you get into Juilliard," Marlene says, nudging my side with her elbow.

I clear my throat. "I didn't get in, actually."

She gasps. "What?"

"I didn't get into Juilliard," I repeat, glancing up at Cole.

"I'm so sorry," he says, tightening his grasp around me.

I shrug. "I just found out right before we came over."

He pulls back to take in my expression. "You don't seem upset, though."

I shrug. "I'm not, really. I mean, I guess I am a little bit."

"Yeah, who needs 'em?" Tess asks as she shoves a plate of freshly cut pizza in my hands.

I laugh genuinely. "That's what I'm thinking."

As we all move to sit down at the table for the second family dinner that was never supposed to happen, Cole holds me back.

"Tess is right, you know. You don't need a school to tell the world what I already know."

"And what's that?" I ask playfully.

He leans down and whispers in my ear, "You're already a star, Alexandra. The brightest among all the constellations."

And I believe him without a doubt.

EPILOGUE

SIX MONTHS LATER

Winters in my home state have always felt cold.

Being in the mountainous region, we endure freezing temperatures and massive amounts of snow and ice.

But winter in New York is an entirely different playing field.

I don't have to remove the ice from my windshield or stay at home when a winter storm rolls through because nothing changes here. Classes still go on, the subways move, and everyone simply braves the elements as they walk through their neighborhoods.

I feel protected by the buildings, even as I stand at the edge of Bryant Park. The snow accumulates on the ground almost gently as I wait for Cole, who was meeting up with Daniel and Madison for coffee after class.

We both spent the fall semester in Pennsylvania. I gave college a true shot while also volunteering and auditioning for theater companies around the city, biding my time until I could get where I really wanted to be.

I ended up applying for the spring term at every school with a theater program in New York and ultimately settled on taking classes at that same film and acting school I saw on that taxi ad.

Cole took a few classes at the community college while doing manual labor at Craig's shop not too far from the Keller house, which led to his getting an offer as a woodworking apprentice up here after Christmas.

He's still a little unsure if he wants to pursue that occupation long-term, and I'm waiting for the right time to corner him about the architecture program brochures I saw in his kitchen last week.

"Hey." Cole walks up to me, a smile tugging at the corner of his mouth before he drops a kiss on mine. "Your nose is freezing."

I laugh and rub it with my glove-clad hand to warm it up. "I love it here, but I definitely preferred meeting up for midnight floats instead of snowy walks."

"If only they had pools in the middle of Manhattan," Cole teases.

"At least I can see the sky from here," I reason as we walk along the sidewalk a little aimlessly.

"So now that you've lived in New York for all of two months, do you think you've gotten a handle on the city?" Cole asks me.

I quirk an eyebrow at his question. "Absolutely not. It's only because of you I haven't ended up at the end of the subway line somewhere in Brooklyn."

He chuckles. "I don't think you've ever given yourself enough credit."

"Maybe," I say. "But that's why I have you, isn't it? To hype me up."

"One of many reasons," he returns with a smirk. "Now come on, there's something I want you to see."

He picks up his pace and leads me down a block before we slip in the side entrance of a white rectangular building. It's beautifully designed, like so many places are here, but it almost has a certain old school grandeur charm.

We walk down a slant, and I take in the massive crowd.

It's definitely been an adjustment, living here around all the noise and the people—it's on another level entirely from the university in Pittsburgh. But at least everyone here is moving with purpose and direction.

"Welcome to Grand Central Station," Cole says.

"Are we going somewhere?" I ask him, staring at the sign that shows the destinations and corresponding track numbers. "New Jersey? Washington, D.C.? Boston?"

"Look up," he encourages.

I do, and I gasp at the sight.

Because on the ceiling of this bustling terminal is such a delicately crafted piece of art, I'm at a loss for words.

The night sky is depicted in a green-blue color with the stars arranged in an interesting presentation, some depicted with the figures they're representing, like Orion hitting Taurus the bull.

"I guess we can come here whenever we want to see the stars," I say, standing on my tip toes to drop a kiss on Cole's mouth.

He smiles. "And we still don't have to play pretend."

BOOKS BY JENNIFER ANN SHORE

Young Adult Romances

Everywhere, Always

Just Play Pretend

Only You in Everything

Perfect Little Flaws

The Extended Summer of Anna and Jeremy

The Stillness Before the Start

Adult Romances

In the Now

Nothing Personal for Breakfast

This Is Your Life

Young at Midnight

"The Islands of Anarchy" Series

New Wave

Rip Current

"The Royally Human Vampire" Series

Metallic Red

Yes, Your Majesty

FREE GIFT FOR YOU!

Want to make your book an autographed copy? Head over to Jennifer's website and get a free bookplate!

https://www.jenniferannshore.com/bookplate

CONNECT WITH JENNIFER

Hi there,

I cannot thank you enough for reading my work. Truly, it means the world to me!

I'd love to connect with you on social media if you're up for it. I'm on all the major social channels, including TikTok (@jenniferannshore) and Instagram (@shorely).

And don't forget to subscribe to my email newsletter (jenniferannshore.com/newsletter) for bonus scenes, new release announcements, giveaways, and more.

All my love! —Jennifer

ACKNOWLEDGMENTS

Writing these thank you notes in this section is a little daunting because even though I've just written thousands of words, it's difficult for me to express how grateful I am for the team who helps make this all go.

Jen, I am so, so, so lucky that we found each other and that you still love me, even though I kill you with my repeated words—that you, in turn murder right back. Thank you for saving my sanity and making my work shine.

Denise, you are such a joy to work with, and I'm so grateful for your nudges and comments that make me smile and laugh and change my books for the better.

Maria, I am so very honored that you gave your creativity to make this beautiful cover. I truly love it, and I'm so happy that you put up with my schedule—and how it turned out!

Lindsay, my dear, you're simply the best. Thank you for your exceptional proofreading skills and appreciation for macarons, even though we have yet to meet up and share a massive plate of them together.

Emily, I'm so grateful for your excitement and final checks on my work—as well as all the smiles I get at your reactions to my distinctly American things. (By the way, if anyone's reading this, they should go check out her debut novel called *Tamara King!*)

Kilroy, my best friend and book photographer, there are NO WORDS for how much I love and appreciate you.

My parents, family, and friends, thank you so much for your support, social shares, and good vibes.

And, finally, but most importantly, to you, dear reader. Without you, these little worlds and books wouldn't exist.

ABOUT THE AUTHOR

Jennifer Ann Shore is an award-winning, bestselling author based in Seattle, Washington.

She writes romance stories that go a little deeper than the standard tropes. Her lineup of more than a dozen books includes standalones, a dystopian series, and a vampire series—with titles such as "Perfect Little Flaws," "Young at Midnight," and "Metallic Red."

Prior to publishing, she led an impressive career in New York, first as a journalist and then as a marketing executive, gaining recognition for her work from companies such as Hearst and SIIA.

Be sure to sign up for her newsletter on her website (https://www.jenniferannshore.com) and follow her on Twitter (@JenniferAShore), Instagram (@shorely), and TikTok (@jenniferannshore).